AMISH WIDOW'S ESCAPE

EXPECTANT AMISH WIDOWS BOOK 11

SAMANTHA PRICE

CHAPTER 1

Not rendering evil for evil, or railing for railing:
but contrariwise blessing;
knowing that ye are thereunto called,
that ye should inherit a blessing.
1 Peter 3:9

BRIDGET LOGAN SLUMPED onto her bed when she'd finished stuffing the last of her late husband's clothes into super-sized garbage bags. She cast her gaze around at the twenty bags that were all going to the Goodwill store. It'd been a mammoth task, packing all of his things, and had she not been moving, she would've left things as they'd always been. He had kept all the mementos from his childhood and Bridget hated throwing some of them out, but his parents hadn't wanted them and she needed to travel light. She reminded herself that his possessions weren't him— she'd always carry Mattie in her heart. He'd been little better than a hoarder, which in a way, made this process easier, but it had given her more things to give away. Their double garage had been so full of sporting equipment that she'd already had two garage sales to lighten the load.

Matthew, or Mattie, as she'd always called him, was gone and now she was alone. They'd been friends from middle school right through to college and they had married ten years ago shortly after graduating.

The only thing that made sense to Bridget right now was to move home to be close to her parents. She'd already signed the papers to get her house onto the market, and the first open house was scheduled for two weeks time. It didn't make sense to keep Mattie's things and move them into storage along with her own possessions. That would be delaying the inevitable process of donating or throwing everything out later on. She kept some photographs and the odd senti- mental keepsake, and everything else had to go.

It had been six weeks since the army personnel had come to her door to inform her that her husband had been killed during his recent deployment to Afghanistan. It had been his fourth tour of active-duty with his unit, and she'd been accustomed to him returning, but when she looked out her window to see a uniformed man and woman heading to her door, she knew there could only be one reason. Mattie had been killed.

Mattie would've approved of her decision to return to their hometown. She'd gone straight from her parents' house to college to getting married, and although she'd been alone during his tours of duty, she'd never lived on her own without knowing that someone was coming home.

In the first few days, she'd drowned her sorrows in alcohol and rocky road ice cream until she hit rock bottom; from there, the only place to go was up.

The weeks passed, and two days ago she threw out the ice cream along with the junk food and poured the remainder of Mattie's wine collection—the bottles that had survived her drinking binge—down the drain.

The removal truck was coming tomorrow and today she was driving his clothes, golf clubs and other sporting goods that hadn't sold in the garage sales to Goodwill. Following that, her next mission had to be cleaning the house from top to bottom. The realtor had advised her to leave some furniture in the house while it was being marketed, as a way to improve appeal, and everything else was going into storage.

BRIDGET GOT out of her car after the long two-day drive between Oklahoma and Pottstown. She stood outside the front of the house and looked up at it. It looked exactly the same as it always had except for the outside paintwork, which looked a little worse for wear than the last time she'd visited.

Her visits to her parents over the last several years had been few. She'd never been particularly close with them, but they had wanted her to come home when they heard about Mattie. When Bridget heard the screen door creak open, she looked to see her mother running out to meet her.

"Oh, Bridget, you poor thing." She wrapped her arms around Bridget.

"I'm alright." Bridget squirmed not entirely comfortable with her mother's embrace since her parents hadn't even made an effort to go to her husband's funeral. Her mother claimed to have some problem where she couldn't leave the house, so naturally, her father couldn't just leave her and go to the funeral either. It might be a genuine psychological problem, but Bridget wondered if it was just more convenient for her mother to stay at home day in and day out.

"You've got Matthew's death benefits at least. Oh, I shouldn't have said that. Forget I said it. Are you okay?" Her mother looked her up and down.

She didn't take too much offense since her mother often blurted out inappropriate things. "I'm doing okay."

"You've lost weight!"

"Believe me I haven't."

"I knew it was a mistake, him joining the army. It

was always a risk that this would happen. Didn't you think about that? He didn't think about you, did he? Just as well you didn't have any children."

"We didn't need any children, Mom, we had Max."

"Is that fleabag still alive?"

It was typical of her mother to call her purebred Persian cat a fleabag. "He's only eight. Cats can live until they're eighteen or twenty, and sometimes even longer."

"Well, where is he?"

"He's in the backseat." Bridget glanced back to the cat-carrier in the car.

"You'll have to keep him in the laundry room. He's not staying in the house. You know I'm allergic."

"I know." Her mother thought she was allergic to everything from dust to pets to anything else she didn't like. Bridget wasn't happy about Max staying in the laundry room. He was used to having the run of the house during the day and always slept on her bed at night. She'd have to sneak him inside at night when her mother went to bed otherwise the poor baby would fret. "Where's Dad?"

"He's playing golf. I've lost your father to golf just as you lost Matthew in the war."

"That's hardly the same thing, Mother." It was typical of her mother to say such insensitive things. Bridget had forgotten what her mother could be like, or maybe she didn't think things through when she'd decided home would be the best place to come. How could she stay here for any length of time? She couldn't. "When will Dad be home?" she asked, not wanting to spend too much time alone with her mother.

"Who can tell? He usually stays out late after a game of golf."

"How often does he play?"

"Nearly every day."

I don't blame him. Bridget nodded thinking her father had chosen a clever way to escape.

"Leave the bags in the car for your father and come inside. Your old room is just the same as it always was. I was going to use it as a sewing room, but I don't do much sewing nowadays."

"Thanks, Mom." She retrieved the cat-carrier from the back seat and headed inside.

"I hope you brought some of that cat litter with you?"

"Yes; it's all in the car."

"Put Max in the laundry room and I'll help you get his things out of the car; the rest we'll leave for your father."

"Thanks, Mom."

When Max was settled in the laundry with his cat bed and litter tray, Bridget went inside to find her mother. She was sitting in the living room, watching a soap opera on TV.

Glancing up at her during an ad, her mother asked, "Would you like something to eat?"

"No thanks. Not right now."

"You have to eat. You're fading away. Have you got bulimia again?"

"No! I never had anything like that. Why do you say things like that?"

"Well, you have to eat."

"I'll get something later." Bridget was quickly hushed as the commercials were over and the latest 'Dr. Heart-throb' had entered the room on the TV. Bridget never watched the daytime soaps, but thought her mother must be watching General Hospital. At the risk of another shushing, she asked, "Aren't you going to talk to me now that I'm here?"

Her mother's hand whipped up like a stop sign. "Shoosh! I'll speak to you when this is over."

Bridget left her mother in the armchair and went to her bedroom. When she pushed the door open, she saw that it was the same as she'd left it. There were her posters on the walls, long forgotten pop stars sporting bad haircuts and out-of-date clothes. On her small desk were all her schoolbooks, still stacked neatly on the edge. "There's no point in keeping these things," she murmured as she walked around and looked at all the things, potent reminders of her childhood.

CHAPTER 2

And the second is like, namely this,
Thou shalt love thy neighbour as thyself.
There is none other commandment greater than these.
Mark 12:31

WITH NOTHING else to do in her old bedroom, Bridget picked up the old diary lying on top of her desk. It was covered in blue material, which Bridget had glued onto the hard cardboard cover. Blue had been her favorite color back then and everything had to be blue. Even the walls of her room had been painted blue and remained so until this day.

She slumped down on the bed and flicked through the tattered worn pages of the well-used diary until she came to a familiar name enclosed in a pink, permanent marker-drawn heart. 'Nat'—his name still made her squirm with disappointment. The way Nat had hurt her was something that she was sure she'd never recover from. She leafed through some more, stopping to read sections here and there of her painful teenage years. With anger welling in her heart, she threw the book of all her secret thoughts across the room with force. It landed on one of the posters and dropped to the floor. Staring at the book, she was surprised that she could still be so hurt about events that had taken place so long ago.

Her mother flung the door open, causing Bridget to jump. With hands on her hips and feet at shoulder-width apart, she stood looking grim. Bridget felt like a naughty child and was transported back to years before.

"What was that thud?" her mother demanded of her.

Reminding herself she was now an adult and answerable to no one she calmly asked, "Has your show finished already, Mom?"

"Yes, it has." Her mother's eyes traveled to the diary on the floor and the poster now hanging askew by one lump of Sticky Tack. "Just because you're in your old room doesn't mean you have to turn into your teenage-self and throw tantrums."

"I never threw tantrums when I was a child."

"I didn't say 'child.' You were perfect and no trouble when you were a child. I said a 'teenager.' You were so difficult to handle back then. Your father and I couldn't say or do anything right. I hope you've changed; I would've thought so."

Bridget sighed. "Sorry, Mom. I just read something that brought back bad memories."

Her mother walked over to the diary, picked it up, closed it carefully, and then placed it back on the desk.

Hoping she might be able to restore their fractured relationship, Bridget tried opening up to her mother. "I didn't have the best of times in school. I was bullied and picked on a lot."

"Just get over it! Suck it up! We've all had to put up with bad behavior from others, but we just forget about them and move on. Something you have to learn to do —that's what adults do."

Bridget sighed. "I'm trying to tell you how I feel."

"I would've thought you'd be upset over your husband more so than upset about reading something in a book."

"I'm upset about Mattie, of course, I am. I'm also upset that awful things happened to me in the past."

"None of us can change the past. It's not worth thinking about."

"I'm still upset by things..."

"Suck it up and get on with it, girl!" Her mother shook her head placing her hands back on her hips and looking down at Bridget who was still perched on the edge of her blue-covered bed.

"Yes, Mother. When did you say Dad would be home?"

"I told you, I'm not sure; he'll likely stay on at the club. Sometimes he doesn't even come home for dinner. He might be earlier since he knows you're coming. We didn't know what time to expect you since you never call on your way when you're visiting."

"The reason I don't call on the way is that you have a habit of calling every ten minutes to ask where I am. It makes me tense." Bridget suddenly realized her mother would've called her in the ad breaks.

"Well, I'm sorry I care," her mother said curtly.

"How come Dad spends so much time at golf. Didn't you play golf?"

"That's your father's thing much more than it was mine. We live separate lives now, pretty much, but don't worry we'd never divorce. He lives his life and I live mine. We're like two people who share a house."

Bridget screwed up her face, but she couldn't say a word against that. Although she had once longed to be in love with someone in a heart-thumping way, her love for Mattie was more friendship than romance. Mattie and she had been dumped by their significant others at the same time. Their bruised egos had found solace in each other's arms—one thing led to another and they ended up married. Bridget had thought she'd been doing the right thing by marrying her best friend. And they'd been happy.

They was no point trying to have a proper conversation with her mother, so Bridget decided to find her father. "I'll go down to the golf club and catch up with him."

"Please yourself, but it's very much a men's thing to do."

"Why don't you come with me? We could both have dinner there with Dad."

She glanced down at her pink slippers. "No. I'll have to get dressed up."

"It's just the local golf club. It's nothing flashy, unless it's changed."

"No, it's still the same. I like being comfortable. You go."

"I'll see if I can find him and bring him home for dinner. How does that sound?"

"Please yourself. I should be able to find some frozen fish in the freezer I can thaw out for dinner. I'll expect you both if I see you. You can always have dinner there with your father if you'd prefer."

"I'll see what happens." Bridget wondered if her mother had remembered that she hated fish or any kind of seafood. Perhaps her mother might prefer that she have dinner at the club with her father.

"Now don't go talking to men. You know what happened the last time you found yourself without a man. You shouldn't jump right into another relationship."

Bridget's jaw dropped open at her mother who hurried back to the TV set. How could her mother say such thoughtless things while she was in so much pain? Mattie hadn't broken up with her—he'd died!

Bridget jumped into her car glad to be getting away from her mother. If things were going to continue like this, coming here was a mistake. The last things she needed were lectures.

When she drove into the parking area of the golf resort, she saw her father's car in the car park. After she had parked as close as she could to his car, she headed into the restaurant/bar area.

Not seeing her father anywhere, she ordered herself a cappuccino, sat down, and looked out the window at the golfers. From where she was, she could only see the driving range and the practice putting area where the beginners were being taught.

She knew if she waited long enough her father would appear. He always had a drink at the end of every game.

When she finished the cappuccino, she went to get another. Then she saw a familiar male figure, but it was too late to turn away because he was smiling and walking toward her. Her heart practically stopped. It was Nat.

CHAPTER 3

And be ye kind one to another,
tenderhearted, forgiving one another,
even as God for Christ's sake hath forgiven you.
Ephesians 4:32

"Bridget! I haven't seen you for years." Her old boyfriend, Nat, held his arms out and when he got close enough, he pulled her close to him. "You're still so beautiful, and I'm glad you kept your hair long."

After the awkward and unexpected embrace, she stepped back, opened her mouth to speak, but no words came out. He was the first man she'd loved before he betrayed her and broke her heart.

"I heard about Mattie, and I'm very sorry. I would've gone to the funeral, but…"

"That's alright. How have you been?"

Nat and she had gone to college together, along with Mattie and Mattie's then girlfriend, Crystal.

"Well, I'm working here now. That says it all." He laughed.

Bridget could see that he was as confident as ever and she had to begrudgingly admit that he was even a little more handsome.

"And I heard you married Crystal?"

"Yes, we got married briefly. Now we're divorced."

"Oh, I'm sorry to hear that." A little part of her was secretly pleased that their relationship had ended in divorce. He'd dumped her to be with Crystal and Crystal had dumped Mattie to be with him.

"Don't be sorry. It was bound to happen. What brings you here?

"I'm back with my parents for awhile until I figure out what to do with myself. I'm selling my house and…" She shook her head. Why was she chatting to this man as though he were some kind of a friend? He wasn't! He had betrayed her trust and she wasn't about to forgive or forget.

Mattie had asked Bridget to find that one true love if anything should happen to him. They both loved each other and would've stayed together. Bridget knew she would never go on a quest to find love, and seeing her old boyfriend again brought that home only too clearly—love was painful and not worth the effort. She'd been right to marry Mattie. Mattie would've never let her down.

"Is everything alright, Bridget?"

"Yes. I would like another cup of coffee."

"Cappuccino?"

"Yes, please."

"Go and sit down; I'll bring it over."

"Thank you." She hurried back to her table by the window glad to get away from him. Had she known he'd been working here, she wouldn't have come looking for her father.

When he brought the coffee over, Bridget was distressed to see that he brought not one but two. He placed both coffees down on the table.

"Mind if I sit down? I'm on my break now."

Bridget didn't know what to say and didn't want to be rude. "I'd prefer to be alone."

He laughed as though she were joking and sat down with her. "I won't be long. There's something I need to say." Nat was just as arrogant as ever.

"Fine," Bridget said in exasperation. After she had brought the hot coffee to her lips, she took a sip.

Nat picked up a packet of sugar, shook it, and then poured it into his coffee with great concentration. She watched as he slowly stirred the sugar into his coffee with a spoon.

He looked up at her. "I guess I owe you an apology."

You certainly do! she thought. "What for?" Bridget asked him.

He chuckled. "For what Crystal and I did to you and Mattie."

"You did us a favor. Mattie and I found each other and married."

Nat stared at her in disbelief. "You're not angry?"

"Not at all."

"And here I've been all these years, worried about seeing you again and what I would say when I saw you."

"Well, you don't need to worry any more."

Nat stared down into his coffee. "I nearly didn't buy the house next door to your parents because of what happened between us."

Bridget nearly dropped her cup, but managed to steady it as she placed it carefully down on her saucer. "Did you say you bought the house next to my parents?"

He nodded. "I've been there nearly a year now."

"They never said anything to me."

"They said they don't hear from you much anymore."

That was true, but something like that warranted telling her right away. Why couldn't they have picked up the phone? They knew what had happened between them.

"Are you still living there now?" she asked, hoping he wasn't.

"Yes. I bought a dog right after the divorce, and I needed a house for the dog. There aren't many apartments around and most of the owners' co-ops wouldn't take a dog. We sold the house we were living in and Crystal got most of it in the divorce—somehow. I could only afford to buy a small house and that's when the house next to your parents came up for sale."

"Do you and Crystal have any children?"

"No, and your parents tell me that you don't either."

Bridget took a deep breath and wished her parents hadn't told her ex-boyfriend everything about her life. "No, we never had any."

"Crystal and I just didn't get around to it."

"How did you end up working here?" she looked around at the large restaurant. Bridget knew it hadn't been in his life plan to work at a golf club serving drinks.

He shrugged his well-muscled shoulders. "I just wanted something without all the pressure."

The last Bridget had heard was that Nat was working as a stockbroker. She could imagine that handling other people's money would be a lot of pressure.

"And what about yourself—what do you do?" he asked.

"I'm a graphic designer. I'm on a few months leave until I settle..."

"Yes, you were always artistic."

"I've got six months leave, but I don't know if I'll go back."

He straightened in his chair. "Are you thinking of staying on here?"

"At this point, I don't know what I'm doing. I'm just taking some time to figure out what to do with the rest of my life."

"Why don't you start by going out to dinner with me tomorrow night?"

She shook her head. "That wouldn't be a good idea."

"Ah, I knew you haven't forgiven me yet."

"I said I'm trying to sort myself out. And I don't want to complicate my life further."

He leaned forward. "Does that mean you still feel some attraction to me?"

"I'm sorry, Nat, but I could never feel anything for another man because I was so in love with Mattie." She couldn't let him think she would ever give him another chance—another chance to break her heart.

"If you're staying at your parents' house, we'll see each other quite a bit. It'll be awkward if we're not friends."

"I don't see why it would be. Anyway, I don't think I'll be at my parents' house for that much longer. It's only a stopover."

"Are you just making this up as you go along?"

She looked around hoping her father would show up. "I came here to see my father. I don't suppose you know how much longer he'll be?"

"They usually stop around five." He looked at his watch. "You don't have much longer to wait."

"Thank you." She took a mouthful of coffee.

Two minutes later, and after more awkward

moments, she was pleased when her father walked in with his golfing cronies. When he spotted her, he hurried over with his arms spread out. She stood up and he swooped her into a tight hug.

"I didn't know you were coming today," he said.

"I told you I would be. Mom knew. Did you forget?"

He shook his head. "I would've stayed home if I knew, or if I'd remembered."

"It doesn't matter. Are you staying here for dinner, Dad?"

He looked over his shoulder at his friends and gave them a signal with his hand to let them know he wouldn't be joining them for a drink. "No, I'll come home for dinner. Do you mind if I have just one drink first?" He looked at Nat, took a seat, and looked back at Bridget. "Hello, Nat."

"Hello, Mr. Dangar."

"Let's go home, Bridget."

"Have a drink on the house, Mr. Dangar. I'll get you one."

"No thank you. Bridget looks tired. I should go home with her. And I told you before, Nat, it's Stan. You're too old to keep calling me Mr. Dangar."

Nat gave a quiet chuckle. "Stan it is."

"Okay," Bridget said to her father in agreement about going home.

Nat sprang to his feet. "I'll see you again soon then, Bridget?"

"I guess so," she said. "Since you now live next

21

door." She glared pointedly at her father who looked away.

On the drive back home, Bridget knew she couldn't stay at her parents' house, not after a few hours with her mother and now especially with Nat living right next door. She was angry with her parents for keeping that from her. They knew how he'd cheated on her while, to her knowledge, he had been in a serious relationship with her.

CHAPTER 4

*By whom also we have access by faith
into this grace wherein we stand,
and rejoice in hope of the glory of God.*
Romans 5:2

AFTER ONE WEEK of staying at her parents' house and doing her best to avoid Nat, Bridget was more than ready to move on. Every day had been the same routine. Her mother would sit in front of the TV most of the day and her father would play golf. Poor old Max was still stuck living in the laundry room and he did not approve of it one bit. Bridget's house had been opened once for an open house, but there'd been no offers. The best thing she could do for her sanity, and

Max's, was to find a place to rent until her house was sold.

With her laptop under her arm, she headed down to the end of the street to the local café to use their Wifi. Bridget often went there to send a few emails to her work colleagues to catch up on the gossip. She tried not to listen to the sad love songs playing, and she hoped they didn't mind her sitting as people ate and then left while she was still there. It was a rustic little café, with more seating outside than inside. As there was a cool breeze, Bridget had taken a seat inside. There were badly painted amateur pictures on the wall with high price tags attached to them, and handmade beaded jewelry in a cabinet against one of the walls. On the other side of the room were a variety of jams, marmalade, teas, and oils for sale. It seemed a community-based café.

Sitting there sipping her cappuccino looking at the real estate offerings in the area, she was disappointed in the rentals. They were all too expensive, and besides that, she would've had to lease them for a whole year. After she had caught up on her emails, she was on her way out of the café when something on the noticeboard caught her eye. In big letters were the words 'for lease, short or long stay.'

She stepped closer to read 'Amish Escape. Small two bedroom cabin available at low monthly rates.' *That's just what I'm after—an escape! A bedroom for me and one for Max.*

Bridget looked at the address. She pulled the notice off the board, sat back down, opened her laptop, and Googled the address to see how far away it was. Up came photographs of the cabin and the local countryside. The interior of the cabin was basic at best, but she didn't need anything more. It was an hour drive away from her parents' house, and more importantly from Nat's house. And she wouldn't give her parents the address so they wouldn't be able to pass it on to Nat.

"Perfect," she murmured as she closed the lid of her laptop. There was no phone number on the flyer and neither could she find any number on the Internet. She would have to drive there and hope that it was still available.

If the cabin were still available, she would take it for three months and if it was gone by the time she got there, she would try to find something similar in the area. She had to get away from her parents, and fast.

By early afternoon, Bridget had the car packed and had told Max they were leaving. Max didn't look too impressed, but Bridget hoped he'd perk up when they arrived at their new place. She told her parents she'd call them and tell them where she was staying once she got settled.

BRIDGET GOT out of the car and knocked on the door of the main house. From there, she could see the cabin and it appeared closed up. It looked like no one was staying there. She hoped she wouldn't have to look for a hotel to spend the night.

An elderly woman finally answered the door. "Hello."

The woman was Amish, as Bridget had expected. She appeared to be in her sixties, a small woman with tanned skin and bright blue eyes. Poking out from the front of her white prayer *kapp* was salt and pepper colored hair.

"Hello." Bridget held out the notice she'd taken from the café. "Is this still available?"

The woman looked down at the piece of paper and then smiled when she looked back at Bridget. "Yes, it is."

Bridget smiled too. "I was hoping it would be free."

The Amish woman's jaw dropped open. "No it's not free; you have to pay to stay there."

Bridget laughed. "I know that. I meant vacant; I should've said that rather than free."

The old lady laughed with her and then told her the price for one month. "And if you want to stay for longer than one month, I'll make it cheaper."

"Yes, please. I'd like to stay for three months if I could." After they had negotiated a price, Bridget asked, "Will a cat be okay, too? He's an older cat and he's no trouble. I'm selling my house and until it sells I'm not sure where to go. And this place looks lovely."

"A cat will be okay. I'm Mrs. Lutz, but you can call

me Ruth. My husband is around somewhere and his name is Jakob."

"I'm Bridget Logan."

"Please to meet you, Bridget Logan. Do you want to have a look at it before you hand over your money?"

"Okay. Best I do that, I guess."

Bridget followed the lady to the house. Ruth unlocked it and stepped back for Bridget to walk through first. It looked just the same as in the photos on her computer.

"Yes, I like it. And it seems very quiet around here and that's just what I need."

"And for the three months?"

"Fine, I'll take it. Will you take a check?"

Ruth shook her head. "Only cash."

"I'll find a bank and come straight back."

"You won't find one open at this time of the day— they'll all be closed. Stay here tonight and then worry about it in the morning. I trust you."

"Oh, thank you. I am a bit tired."

"Have you eaten?"

"Yes, I got something on the way here."

"Good. There are tea and coffee in the pantry and I'll bring you back some milk and bread to see you through the night. You'll have to go to town to get supplies if you didn't bring any with you, but whenever you're desperate for something, there's a small general store where you can pick up a few odds and ends."

"Thank you."

27

The old lady handed her the key.

Bridget brought her things in from the car and by the time she had unpacked, Ruth reappeared with a small jar of milk and some bread.

"Thank you. That's very kind of you, Ruth."

"If you need anything, I'm not far away." Ruth went on to explain that the cabin had electricity even though the main house she lived in had none. She'd also mentioned that there was a phone in the barn that Bridget could use. Apart from those few modern conveniences, there was no air conditioner, no television and no Internet connection. Bridget figured she could live without those for a while. She still had her mobile phone and could connect to the Internet through that if need be.

"Thank you. I'll get the money tomorrow and pay up the three months."

Ruth smiled and nodded. "Very good. I'll see you tomorrow."

The first thing Bridget did when Ruth had gone was close all the doors and windows and let Max out of his cat-carrier. "This is only temporary, Max. Soon, we'll have another home. It'll be a new start for you and me."

Max ignored her while he sniffed and explored every inch of the cabin.

"Don't be critical, Max. It's better than the laundry room."

Max ignored her and kept going on his mission of checking the place out.

Bridget settled into the couch. At least she was away from Nat and his clumsy attempts to make things up to her. She would've welcomed his attention and his apologies immediately after everything had happened, but well over ten years after the fact was far too late.

THE DAYS PASSED and Bridget often talked with Ruth of a morning, as Ruth worked in the garden and the vegetable patch.

Today she was on her morning walk and spotted Ruth planting seedlings.

"Good morning, Ruth."

"How are you today, Bridget? Off on another walk?"

"Yes, I'm getting a little exercise. It was either this or yoga and I don't fancy yoga." She looked at the tiny green plants Ruth was pushing into the soft dark earth. "Are they tomato seedlings?" Before Ruth could answer, a wave of nausea swept over Bridget and she lost her breakfast right there, in front of Ruth and all over the seedlings.

Ruth pushed herself to her feet and stretched out a hand toward her. "Are you ill?"

Bridget wiped her mouth with the back of her hand. "I'm sorry. I must've eaten something that disagreed with me." She shook her head, wondering why it had happened. "It could be food poisoning."

"Did you eat out yesterday?"

"No, I ate my own cooking, but I'm not a very good cook."

"But you were sick a couple of days ago, too."

"That's right." Bridget put her hand on her stomach. "I was nauseous the other morning. It could be stomach flu."

"I'll help you back to the cabin."

Bridget accepted Ruth's help since she was like a caring old aunt.

Once they were in the cabin, Ruth ordered Bridget to sit down. "I'll fix you a cup of tea."

Bridget was too sick to tell her she didn't feel like tea or anything else. All she wanted was for the nausea to go away.

"You haven't got anything in your fridge. I'm looking for milk and you don't have any."

"I don't have milk in my tea. I'm not really a milk drinker."

"You don't have anything else in your fridge either."

"I'm going shopping later today. I'll pick up more food."

Ruth closed the fridge door and shook her head as she stared at Bridget. "You're in no condition to go anywhere. I'll bring you some food."

"No, you don't have to go to that trouble. I'll be okay. I never get sick."

"It's no trouble. Now, I'll make tea for you. I don't know how you can drink tea without milk."

"That's the way I've always had it "

"The tea should settle your stomach."

"I don't know. Many things don't agree with me lately."

"I don't mean to pry, but do you think you could be expecting?"

"You mean pregnant?"

Ruth nodded.

"No. I mean, I don't think so." Bridget put her fingertips to her lips. "I suppose it's possible, but I could be like this because of all the stress." Bridget had previously shared with Ruth how her husband had recently died. "We weren't trying—my husband and I, but I guess neither were we trying not to get pregnant."

"Oh, I'm sorry I didn't mean to pry; that's not any of my business."

"Do you think I could be?" She added up the months in her head. If she were pregnant, she would be five months already. Bridget answered her own question, "No, I don't think so."

Ruth's bright blue eyes twinkled. "But it's a possibility?"

"One chance in a thousand."

"Then there is more chance of you being pregnant than you winning the lottery. And someone always wins the lottery."

Ruth turned away from her to fill the kettle up with water. When the tea was made, Ruth sat next to her while she drank it.

SAMANTHA PRICE

"Feeling better?"

"A little, a little better."

"Do you have any dry crackers?"

"No. I don't have anything like that."

"I'll bring some things back with me. You stay right there."

"I don't want you to go to any trouble."

"It's no problem at all. I enjoy doing things for people."

Mattie and she had no great desire to have children and when they hadn't become parents in the first few years of marriage, she became convinced they'd be one of those couples who weren't able to conceive.

When Ruth left after fussing over her and bringing her back different kinds of food and herbs that were supposed to relieve her symptoms, Bridget walked around in the fresh air just outside the cabin. What would she do if she had become pregnant? The timing couldn't be worse. She could probably still keep her job and work part time from home, if her boss agreed to that. Bridget had been wearing dresses lately because her jeans had become too tight. Maybe it wasn't just bloat from eating too much salty food—she could be pregnant. It was possible.

LATER THAT DAY, Ruth returned to Bridget's cabin. "How are you feeling now?

"Much better, thank you so much; you're very kind."

"Come to the house for dinner tonight."

"Are you sure that would be alright with Jakob?" Bridget had only met Jakob a couple of times. He seemed to be friendly enough, but he was a man of few words.

"Of course; he loves having people over for dinner."

"Yes, I'd like that, but I don't know if I'll be that hungry."

"If that's the case, you don't have to eat too much. The company might be a nice distraction for you. It can't be good to be on your own so much."

Bridget nodded and wondered if she should point out that she wasn't alone because Max was there. And not only that, she'd chose the peace and quiet of being alone because that's what she needed. Then again, she didn't want to sound like a mad cat lady. Was she turning into one?

"Dinner will be at six thirty, but come over anytime after six."

Bridget nodded at the kindly Amish woman. "Thank you, I'll be there."

When Ruth left, she put her alarm on for five and went to bed with a book that she'd gotten out of the library a couple of days before.

CHAPTER 5

A new commandment I give unto you,
That ye love one another; as I have loved you,
that ye also love one another.
John 13:33

RUTH OPENED the door of her house and showed Bridget into the living room.

When Bridget walked in, she was surprised to see that there was an Amish man sitting down and he wasn't Jakob. He appeared to be in his late thirties. The man bounded to his feet and Bridget was impressed by his height and his large warm smile. The only thing was, Bridget wasn't feeling well enough to make small talk with people she didn't know. She'd thought it was just going to be Ruth and Jakob.

He introduced himself. "I'm Daniel Lindenlaub, but please just call me Dan—everyone does. My father was called Daniel too and it got very confusing, so everyone has called me Dan for as long as I can remember."

"Okay. It's nice to meet you, Dan."

"Ruth tells me you've been ill?"

"It's nothing, just the stomach flu, I'm sure. I'm better now, though. I don't think I'm contagious." Bridget managed a laugh as she sat down on the couch.

Once Dan sat back down, Ruth walked to the kitchen leaving them alone.

Jakob then came into the room, saving Bridget from having to think of something to say. After she had exchanged greetings with Jakob, Dan spoke again.

"What brings you here, Bridget?"

The small talk had started already. Bridget silently reminded herself to be patient. She took a deep breath; she had to go through with the mind-numbing talk with strangers when she preferred to be home curled up with her cat and a good book. "I've come here for a quiet time, to gather my thoughts and make some plans. My husband died just a few months ago and I'm reassessing my life." It was too heavy a topic for dinner conversation, but the man had asked.

He gave a sad smile. "I'm sorry to hear that; it must be very hard for you."

"I'm adjusting. Do you live close by?" She asked Dan the question to get the attention away from herself.

"I live down the road not too far from here."

Jakob butted in, "Dan has never married despite all Ruth's attempts to match him up with women." Jakob chuckled for a moment at his personal insight into his wife and his friend.

"Is that what she does?" Bridget asked.

The two men laughed when they looked at each other. Somehow Bridget guessed that Dan would've taken things a little more seriously.

"Bridget was living in Oklahoma with her husband, and her family home is in Pottstown only an hour's drive away from here," Jakob told Dan.

"Ah, it's very nice in Oklahoma, I hear."

"It's very nice here, too. I've been staying here for a few weeks now and I like it. It's quiet with the beautiful countryside. I never thought I'd like it, for some reason, but it's a welcome change."

"Bridget is a graphic designer," Ruth said.

He looked back at Bridget. "I don't know what that is but it sounds impressive."

"I believe that's it's something to do with computers?" Ruth commented.

Bridget nodded. "That's right, and designing. Art work, printing, and stuff." It was too complicated to tell them in a few words exactly what her job entailed.

"That could be useful, Dan. Didn't you want help with that website for your rocking horses?" Ruth asked.

"Yes, I do. If you weren't taking a break right now,

Bridget, I might have become a customer—that is if you took on small customers like me."

Just when she had her mouth open to respond, Ruth said sharply, "Bridget is taking a break."

Dan frowned and straightened his back. "Yes, I know. Forgive me. I wasn't dropping a hint or anything."

Bridget smiled and felt a little uneasy. Was Ruth annoyed with Dan for asking, or was she protecting Dan from spending time with her? If so, why had Ruth mentioned his website? "I could take a look at where you're at and point you in the right direction, Dan."

"I'd really appreciate that."

"You make rocking horses for a living?"

He laughed. "I know it sounds a little shocking. Most people think I do it in my spare time, but it's my only income."

Jakob interrupted, "Meaning, he makes a good living from it. He's very successful."

"I don't know about that," Dan said, "I put a lot of effort into it, and I work all day every day, except Sundays of course. We do as little work as possible on Sundays."

"Because the seventh day God rested?" Bridget remembered that from the days when she went to church as a youngster.

Jakob answered, "That's right."

"How fascinating. I'd like to see some of your

38

rocking horses. I've always liked them—I did when I was a child."

"Go and have a look at his store," Jakob said.

"You have an actual store full of rocking horses?"

"I do."

"Wow!"

Dan chuckled. "A rocking horse was something I always wanted as a child and my father was good with his hands, but he was always too busy to make me one. It didn't stop me hoping every birthday and Christmas that I'd get one."

"So this is you playing out your childhood dreams?"

"I think so."

Dan and she shared a laugh.

"I'll let you in on a secret, then. I always wanted one as a child too, but never got one either. To me, they represent happy times and there was always something special about them."

"Were you raised in a large family?" Dan asked.

"It's only me. How about you?"

"I've got too many brothers and sisters to count."

"How many is that exactly?"

"There were fourteen of us, and I was the seventh child."

"Fourteen? I wonder how your mother coped? Mine could barely cope with me."

"We all pitched in. The older ones took care of the younger ones. It wasn't as hard as you might think, but there's a much longer story attached to all that."

Bridget couldn't even begin to think of what it would be like to have so many children or to be raised in a family of fourteen. "I'm looking forward to seeing your rocking horses."

He pushed his dark hair back from his face. "I hope you're not disappointed."

Jakob swiped his hand through the air. "I think you'll be impressed, Bridget. Don't listen to him."

Over the dinner table that evening, Bridget started to warm to Dan. Now she was pleased he'd been there for dinner; he was just as friendly as Ruth and Jakob.

"Just tell me where you want to meet and we can go over things for your website. I'd be only too happy to help," Bridget said.

"I'll give you the address of the store before I leave."

"Okay. I'll come there tomorrow and then we can set up a time to go over the ideas you have for your website."

"Thank you. That's very kind of you."

"You'll be at the store tomorrow?"

"Do you want me to come with you, Bridget?" Ruth asked.

"No, I'll be able to find it by myself. I've got GPS on my phone."

"It's not hard to find. It's on the corner of Bridge and Market Streets. It's only a small store. I have the storefront out front and I've got a workshop at the back of it."

"I can't wait to see it and all your horses."

He laughed. "Don't get too excited or you could be disappointed. I've got eleven different styles and I take orders from them if someone wants something slightly different. Sometimes people will want different colors, or their children's names carved into the saddles."

Before Bridget left Ruth's house, she'd made arrangements to meet Dan in his store at eleven the next day. As Bridget wandered across the yard to her cabin, she was pleased with herself for making the effort to go to Ruth and Jakob's place for dinner against her better judgment. More than that, she was pleased that she was getting over the stomach flu, and hopefully, that was all it was.

WHEN BRIDGET WOKE the next morning, she felt fine. After she had dressed and made herself some toast, she went out into the garden for her morning walk. She'd made that her ritual, a walk in the cool fresh air every morning.

As she walked, she wondered about the Amish and their beliefs. She'd always thought they would be closed off and non-communicative with people who weren't Amish, but they'd been lovely to her.

When she was at the usual halfway mark and was just about to turn back to head to the cabin, another wave of nausea gripped her stomach. She heaved up behind a tree. She finished, and then looked around hoping that Ruth wasn't somewhere watching. Ruth was nowhere to be seen, but her words from the previous day rang through her head. What if she were pregnant? It was quite possible, even though unlikely.

She decided to find a doctor in town as soon as she had finished her visit with Dan.

CHAPTER 6

Every valley shall be exalted, and every mountain and hill shall be made low: and the crooked shall be made straight, and the rough places plain:
Isaiah 40:4

BRIDGET FOUND Dan's store later that morning and parked as close to it as she could. It was odd to make friends with Amish people. She was certain they didn't usually mix with people they considered outsiders.

Dan's store was on a corner and had two large display windows where he had four big rocking horses, and some smaller ones at their hooves.

"Hello, Bridget. I must apologize for last night."

Bridget looked over at Dan who was standing just outside the door of his shop.

He continued as he walked closer, "I had no idea that Ruth would volunteer your services for the website."

Bridget giggled. "She does have a way about her. Something tells me she always gets what she wants. I truly don't mind."

He laughed. "Thank you. I had no idea which way to go."

"I'm thankful for having something to do today."

"Well, if you could point me in the right direction, I would appreciate it."

Bridget nodded and looked into his brown eyes. "Should we start by you showing me around your store?"

"Of course. Follow me." Dan walked back into the store and then showed Bridget through, introducing her to each of his rocking horse designs.

"They're so unique. Each one has its own personality and they're so well made."

"Thank you."

She ran her fingers through a horse's mane. "Is this real horse hair?"

"Yes, it is. All the hair's real and all the saddles and bridles are just like the real ones, made out of leather. They're as authentic as they can be."

"They're so lovely. What did you have in mind for the website?"

"Come through to the workshop, so we can sit down."

Dan took her through to the back room, which was his workshop. There were wood shavings scattered on the floor underneath a long gray workbench that ran down the center of the shop. Various tools of different shapes and sizes were spaced evenly, hung on the two side walls.

He looked around. "You can see I don't often get visitors." He pulled up a chair for her and then perched himself on the edge of the workbench. "To answer your question, the only thought I had was to show each design and the individual prices. Beyond that, I have no idea."

"Do you have photographs of the horses?"

He shook his head. "No, I don't."

"That's the first place we'll need to start."

"I've got a friend with a camera."

Bridget shook her head. "You'll need professional shots."

He grimaced. "That sounds expensive."

"It doesn't have to be, but you will have to spend money on the website before it's finished. You have to spend money to make money sometimes."

"I know that and I'm willing to do that."

He looked so helpless that she added, "I can look into it for you. If you haven't even made a start."

"Please do. I'm grateful and I'll pay you for your time here today as well as for any time you spend on helping me."

"That's not necessary. I offered. It'll give me something to do other than read and go for my morning walks. I don't have much to do until my house sells."

"You're very gracious. The truth was that you were volunteered, if you remember correctly, by Ruth."

Bridget laughed. "I can't remember how it happened. It'll keep my hand in. My boss will thank you. I'll find a local photographer. What's your time-frame for getting the website up and running?"

"I've got no time in mind. It's something I've been thinking of for the past few years, so I'm in no rush. The sooner the better, business-wise, I guess."

"I'll start making some calls this afternoon."

"Excellent." He rubbed his large hands together. "How about a cup of coffee?"

Bridget's eyes flickered around the workshop, wondering how he was going to make coffee. There was no kitchenette, as far as she could see, and no electric kettle anywhere—not even a small fridge.

When she didn't answer right away, he said, "I'll get it from the café next door. I'm afraid I don't even boil hot water here."

"I'd love a cappuccino."

"Coming up, but you'll have to mind the store for me." He raised his eyebrows waiting for an answer.

"Deal."

"I won't be too far away if you get a customer." He jumped off the workbench and headed out the door.

She stood up and studied all the pieces of wood that he'd been working on. Then, she headed over to his desk in the far corner of the room. On top of the desk were utility bills and handwritten notes.

She turned around and looked out into the store. Seeing no one about, she picked up one of the notes and read it. It was a letter from a woman called Deirdre. She spoke of her vacation at her Aunt Molly's house. Reading between the lines, it was clear to see that this woman liked Dan.

Bridget was suddenly overcome with sadness over Mattie being gone. Her eyes filled with tears. He'd been her friend, and the only person who really understood her and had stood by her. Mattie had been closer to her than anyone and now he was gone. She sniffed back the tears. If only there were some way to tell him how much she missed him, or if she could talk to him one more time—just one more time. She'd never even said a proper goodbye. He'd left for the deployment while she was at work. A tear trickled down her cheek.

She wiped her eyes quickly when she heard someone coming into the store. Expecting to see Dan coming back with two coffees, she was shocked to see an Amish woman.

"Hello," Bridget said stepping from the backroom into the store.

"Uh, hello. I was looking for Dan."

Bridget wondered if this woman was Deirdre. "He's just next door, in the coffee shop. He'll be back in a minute."

"Oh, thank you." The quiet-spoken woman gave her a smile and hurried outside.

Bridget watched the woman head in the direction of the coffee shop.

Five minutes later, Dan came back into the store.

"Someone came looking for you," Bridget said.

"Yes, she came into the café while I was getting the coffees."

"I hope she didn't get the wrong idea."

He handed her a coffee. "About what?"

He frowned and Bridget immediately felt silly for thinking that the Amish woman might see her as some kind of threat. Dan would only be interested in an Amish woman. "I'm sorry, I just thought she might be…"

He laughed. "She's a friend and nothing more."

Bridget wondered if the young woman might have wanted something more. She had looked fairly anxious to see Bridget in the store rather than Dan.

"You don't believe me?" he asked in his usual relaxed and friendly manner.

"Of course, I do. I've just got a lot on my mind. Things have been a bit weird lately."

"I can imagine they would be. Is there anything that I can do?"

"You're helping me already by giving *me* something to do."

He took a mouthful of coffee. "Glad to be of help. I'd still like to pay you for your trouble."

She shook her head. "I don't need the money." She lifted up the take-out container. "I'll take the coffee as payment."

"That's a good deal for me."

She laughed.

While she drank her hot drink, he told her a little more about his designs and what made his different from many other rocking horses.

Bridget left the store an hour later with a good sense of his business and what he wanted to achieve from the website.

Before she did anything about finding a photographer, she drove down the main street looking for a doctor. Four blocks down, she found one.

The doctor was able to see after a fifteen-minute wait.

"ARE YOU SURE?"

"Positively sure. One hundred percent." The doctor stared at her through his thick-rimmed glasses.

She breathed out heavily as her eyes darted around the room.

"Is there someone I can call for you?"

"No. My husband died recently and this is the last thing I expected. Although, I should've realized much sooner what was going on. I haven't been eating much and I've been putting on weight all the same. And… other things."

"Do you want me to refer you to an obstetrician?"

She stared at the doctor. "I'm in the middle of selling my house in Oklahoma. I don't know where I'll be in a few months."

"Now might be a good time to start making some decisions."

She nodded. "Yes, you're right. Yes, please give me some names."

Bridget drove back to the cabin in no state to figure out what she was going to do. She wasn't upset, she wasn't happy; she was too much in shock to feel anything but numb.

CHAPTER 7

And Jesus answering saith unto them,
Have faith in God.
Mark 11:22

BRIDGET SAT down at her small kitchen table wondering what she would do. According to the doctor, it was real—she was going to have a baby. Now there was another person and another life to consider in her plans for the future. Her doctor was right, now was the time to make some decisions. Bridget fished her mobile phone out of her bag and called the realtor to see how close the house was to selling.

"I'm sorry, Bridget, the market's in a slump."

"Still?" The realtor gave her the same story she'd heard before.

"You might get a quicker sale if you staged the house with some more modern furniture."

"I left furniture in the house."

"Yes, I know, but many people like a different kind of furniture. Yours is… well, yours is not the kind that people imagine themselves living with."

Bridget frowned. The realtor was telling her that she and Mattie had bad taste. "We liked it."

"All the same, it will make the house more appealing to buyers, and the garden is starting to need attention."

"I could call a gardener to mow the lawn and do some tidying up."

"We have a man for that. We can add that onto the selling price of the house to save you some upfront money."

"Yes, I'd appreciate that. How much would staging cost?"

"Generally around fifteen thousand."

The phone nearly dropped out of Bridget's hand. "Fifteen thousand dollars?"

"Yes. We don't want to skimp."

"Is the furniture gold plated or something?"

The realtor laughed. "Most houses sell quickly after they're staged, but I'm afraid that'll have to be an upfront cost to you."

Bridget held her head. "I just don't have that kind of money at this time. The person who buys it will have to have my bad taste in furniture."

"Oh, Bridget, I didn't mean you had bad taste. It's just that it's not contemporary and up-to-date —on trend. Buyers don't have much imagination and there's a lot of competition out there at the moment."

"Well, how long do you think before it sells?"

"I think we have to meet the market."

"What does that mean?"

"I think we need to lower the price."

"But that's the price you suggested. I thought it should be listed lower in the first place."

The realtor gave a laugh. "I might have been carried away because I like the house so much."

Bridget was growing a little annoyed. Dropping the price of the house wasn't something she thought she'd have to do until she was in negotiation with buyers. "How much do you think I'll have to drop?"

"Why don't we try ten thousand dollars? That will bring it down into the next price bracket."

"Do you think that will make a difference?"

"Yes, it'll bring it into the next lower search price on the Internet and that's where we're getting most of our buyers at the moment."

Bridget sighed and considered moving back into the house, but then she'd be continually reminded of Mattie. "Okay, lower it, but the buyers will have to look past my bad taste."

"Oh, Bridget, you're so funny."

"Not really."

"I'll make the changes now and get the gardener out there."

Bridget nodded and then realized that the realtor couldn't hear a nod. "Okay, thanks."

When she hung up the phone, she hoped she was doing the right thing. There was no way she could pay money for the staging, but she felt awful dropping the price without knowing where she'd end up when she eventually sold.

Bridget was jolted out of her daydreams when she heard a knock on her still open front door. She turned to see Ruth standing there.

"Ruth, come in." She stood up to greet her.

"How are you? I saw you come back in your car and you didn't look too happy. I hope I'm not prying, but did you see Dan today like you'd arranged?"

"Yes, I did. Do you have time to sit with me?"

"I do."

Once they were seated, Bridget asked, "Would you like a cup of tea or coffee?"

"No, thank you. I've just had one not long ago."

Bridget took a deep breath. "I saw Dan and I worked out how I can help him. I'm arranging a good photographer and then we'll take things from there."

"I appreciate your help with Dan. He's a good friend." Ruth looked closer into Bridget's face. "Is there something troubling you?"

Bridget nodded and a large lump formed in her

throat. She coughed. "I found out that I'm pregnant, just like you thought."

Ruth leaned forward and seized Bridget's hand. "That's wonderful news. I'm so happy for you." When she saw the look on Bridget's face, she tightened the grip on her hand. "Aren't you happy about it?"

"The truth is that I don't know how I feel. It was so completely unexpected, and now I'll have to get used to the idea. I mean, it's not ideal. I never saw myself as a single parent. It's not fair to the child." *And not fair to me.* "I'm sure it won't be easy to do it all myself either."

"What about your family—your parents? Won't they help?"

Bridget smiled. "They had trouble enough raising me. I don't think they'll be happy about me raising a child alone. Maybe they will, but they won't be any help—no help at all. All my mother wants to do is watch TV and my father plays golf every day. I don't think they like children. I was an inconvenience to them, so I think a grandchild will be the same."

"That's too bad. Do you have any close women friends?"

"I don't make friends too easily. I have people I work with, but they're 'work friends.' In my experience, if I were to leave work they'd eventually stop calling and emailing me. That's just how it is."

"So you're alone?"

Bridget blinked hard as tears stung behind her eyes.

She didn't want one tear to fall because she knew she wouldn't be able to stop crying. "I've got Max."

"Who's Max?"

Smiling, Bridget pointed to Max who was asleep on the couch. "That's Max."

Ruth giggled. "Oh, Max is the cat. You're not alone, then."

"I'll feel better once I sell my house. I'll buy a little place somewhere where my child and I will be happy."

"That's the way—happy thoughts."

"Are you sure you don't want a cup of hot tea?"

Ruth remained silent, stood up and walked to the fridge, opened it and looked inside. "No food again?"

"I forgot to get some. I meant to."

Ruth closed the fridge and shook her head. "Bridget, you must look after yourself. You're eating for two now."

"Yes, I know. I will from now on. I will."

"I'll bring a cooked meal over to you."

"No, please don't. You've done so much already. The shops are still open I'll go and get food."

"You can do that tomorrow. I'll bring you a hot dinner and some food for snacks. You must be sure to eat. That baby needs food to grow properly. Now get on that couch and put your feet up. Max will have to move." Ruth put her hand under Bridget's arm.

Bridget stood up and watched Ruth clap her hands near Max's head. He jumped off the couch and started walking toward the door. Bridget beat Max to the door and closed it.

"Now lie down and put your feet up, Bridget."

Bridget did as she was told while Ruth disappeared into the bedroom. She came back out with a blanket and covered her with it.

"I saw a book in the bedroom. Would you like to read it now?"

"That would be perfect."

Ruth brought the book out and then left her alone. Bridget glanced at Max who was now sitting on the easy chair staring at her with his large green eyes. "I'm sorry, Max. It wasn't me. You can come back up here if you want. There's enough room." Max didn't move, but kept glaring at her in obvious disgust at being replaced on the couch.

Bridget flipped through the book to find her place. Ruth was very motherly and she wondered why her mother couldn't have been like that. Her mother was too worried about missing anything on television to be concerned with her.

CHAPTER 8

There is no fear in love; but perfect love casteth out fear:
because fear hath torment.
He that feareth is not made perfect in love.
1 John 4:18

THE NEXT MORNING after Bridget's walk, she waited until after nine o'clock and then booked a visit to an obstetrician. The soonest they could fit her in, once she gave the receptionist her approximate due date, was three weeks away.

Bridget was left feeling in limbo with no direction until her house sold. Once it sold she'd be able to make plans. Worried about money, she called Trevor, her boss. After she had told him her situation, he agreed that she could work from home on a contractual basis once she was able. Now she would be working for herself, but he guaranteed her all the work she could handle, which gave her some peace of mind. She wondered how long it would take for her widow's pension paperwork to be processed by the military.

There were two things she had to do today: fill the fridge to keep Ruth happy, and then find a good photographer for Dan. Dan's website project would keep her mind occupied while she waited the three weeks to see the obstetrician.

She packed her laptop and headed into town to find somewhere that had Wifi so she could source a suitable photographer.

WHILE BRIDGET ATE a slice of frosted cinnamon cake in a small café close to Dan's store, she browsed the websites of local photographers and looked at samples of their work. When she found the one she thought would suit, she pulled out her mobile phone and made a call. The photographer was free that very afternoon, so Bridget set up an appointment for later that day for him to meet with herself and Dan at Dan's store.

When she finished her coffee and cake, Bridget hurried up the road to see Dan, hoping that the time she arranged would suit.

When Bridget walked into the rocking horse shop,

she saw the same woman in the store that had come in the day before.

Dan had been talking to the woman, and then he looked at Bridget. He seemed pleased to see her.

"Bridget, hello! Have you met Deirdre?"

"Yes, sort of, but we didn't exchange names; hello again."

The woman nodded at her and gave a smile. "I won't keep you, Dan. I'll see you soon, though?"

Dan nodded. "I'll see you soon."

When the woman left the store, Bridget said, "I'm sorry, I hope I didn't interrupt anything."

"No, nothing. Nothing at all."

"Well, I'm hoping you're free at three o'clock today."

"I don't close until five."

"I know that, but I've made an appointment for a photographer to meet us here at three for an initial consultation."

"Yes, that's fine. That's great. You move fast."

"I told you, you're giving me something to do. The website is a good distraction for me."

He smiled. "I'm glad that you're being helped by helping me. Although, I think I'm getting the better end of the deal."

She laughed. "I don't know about that."

He glanced at the clock on the wall. "Do you want to wait here until then?"

"No, I don't want to be under your feet all that time. I'll come back at three."

"Are you sure? I've got some sanding you'd be able to help me with, and then you could do some glazing, or possibly braid some horse's hair?" he joked.

She laughed. "I would certainly wreck each and every one of those things. I've never been good with my hands."

"Thank you for all your help, Bridget. I truly had no idea where to start."

"Don't thank me yet. We're a long way away from you having a website up and running. The photography is only the first step. I can register you a name for your website if you'd like."

"Great! I haven't done that yet."

"We'll run through those things later. I won't hold you up now." Bridget left the store feeling satisfied that she was helping someone as nice as Dan.

She had three hours to fill in, so she decided to go to the supermarket. On the walk there, she came across a baby goods store. She stopped still in front of the window and imagined what it would be like to soon have a tiny person who would fit into such miniscule clothes. In a short space of time, her life would be turned upside down. She didn't know anything about babies; she'd have to learn fast. Before she knew what she was doing, she found her feet were walked up the two steps of the store.

"Good morning!" a bright and breezy sounding

woman called out as she walked toward Bridget.

"Hello. Mind if I have a look around?"

"Certainly. Are you looking for a gift?"

Bridget shook her head. "I'm looking for myself."

"Oh, congratulations. You're not even showing."

Bridget looked down at her stomach. "Thank you. It's still early days."

"Is it your first?"

"It is."

"That's why you look so small. You'll be bigger sooner with the second. Have a look around and let me know if I can help you with anything."

"Thank you."

The sales girl left her to wander by herself through the racks of clothing. Bridget picked up the tiny clothes envisioning a baby small enough to fit into them. A million thoughts ran through her mind. As well as telling her parents about the baby, she'd have to tell Mattie's mother and father. It was too soon to buy anything and with the house not being sold yet and having paid for three months accommodation, she had to watch every cent. After having a good look at all the items she'd eventually need, she said goodbye to the sales girl and left the store, feeling a little excited about having a baby.

Bridget headed to the supermarket where she filled her cart with food, paid for it, headed back to the cabin, put things away, and got to Dan's store in time for the appointment with the photographer at three.

CHAPTER 9

For I have said, Mercy shall be built up for ever:
thy faithfulness shalt thou establish in the very heavens.
Psalm 89:2

DAN AND BRIDGET sat with the photographer, Peter Langley. He'd had a good look at Dan's rocking horses and then he'd showed them his portfolio. He gave them some ideas on how to display the horses for the photos. Peter wanted Amish farmland and barn backgrounds for the horses and when Dan gave him the go ahead for the job, he asked Dan to line up the locations to save time and money.

The photographer had come in and left, and it had all been like a whirlwind.

"I think he'll be good," Bridget said.

"Yes, I think so too. Thanks for finding him. I'm sure it'll expand my business, being able to have my horses on the Internet. Many other Amish businesses are on the Internet now."

"Everyone has to be these days. Can you handle the extra work if you get a big order?"

"I can find extra workers if need be. I've had different people work for me from time to time. I've got all my pieces documented in a book, piece by piece much like a recipe for each different design."

"That's good. You can have some kind of production line."

He laughed. "That's my idea of how I've always wanted things to be. I don't know if I'll ever get there. I'm hoping to."

"We've all got to have hope."

"Have dinner with me tonight?"

"Have you been talking with Ruth?"

"What, about you?"

Bridget nodded.

"No."

"Oh." Bridget giggled. "I thought she might have said something about no food in my fridge."

"Then you must have dinner with me."

"I've just done a big lot of grocery shopping."

He frowned. "Is that a no?"

"I would like to have dinner with you. Thank you."

"I'll collect you at seven?"

"Perfect. Although, will it be in a buggy?"

"Yes."

"How about I meet you somewhere instead?"

"You don't like buggies?"

She was worried that the ride in a buggy might make her queasy, but didn't want to tell him that. "I've never been in one. I'd prefer to meet you somewhere."

"Come with me." He walked to his storefront window and when she stood next to him, he pointed to a restaurant across the road. "Best food in the area."

"Okay, shall I meet you at seven?"

He nodded. "Yes."

She walked out of his store feeling as though she'd had a productive day, and she was looking forward to spending more time with Dan. There was something about being around him that made her feel good.

When she got home, she parked her car and was heading to the cabin when she saw Ruth walking toward her. "Hello, Ruth."

"Hello. How are you feeling?"

"I'm feeling much better today. I'm starting to get used to the idea of having a baby—not totally, but I'm getting there."

Ruth laughed. "You'll be a good mother."

"Thank you. I need encouragement."

"How are you doing for food? Have you been shopping today?"

"Yes. I went earlier and you'll be pleased to know my fridge is stacked and even Max has enough food to

SAMANTHA PRICE

last for weeks." It felt good to have Ruth watching over her.

"It's not Max I'm concerned about. How about I bring you over another hot meal tonight. I always make more than the two of us can eat."

"Oh thank you, but that's not necessary. I'm having dinner with Dan."

Her face darkened. "Dan? Just the two of you?"

"Yes."

She frowned and her mouth closed tightly.

"Is there something wrong with that?"

Ruth scratched the side of her face and looked thoughtful. "An Amish man won't marry a woman who isn't Amish."

"What?" Bridget couldn't control her laughter, but had to stop when Ruth was still looking most serious. "No. It's not like that at all. I helped him find a photographer today and I think it's just his way of saying thanks. That's all. I'm not trying to find a husband and he's not trying to find a wife."

"Just remember that Amish men take finding a wife very seriously. There's no divorce and to have a happy home to raise children in, the husband and wife need to get along. Sometimes a couple think they get along, but once they live together they can't stand each other. That's what happened to a friend of mine and now she and her husband live in separate houses because there's no divorce."

68

"I'll remember that, but I'm not looking for anything like that. That's the last thing on my mind."

"Don't you want a father for the baby?"

"Well, that would've been preferable, but my baby's father has gone and I had no choice in it. All I can do is the best I can do with what I've got."

"Most women in your situation would be hunting down a man."

Bridget smiled at the dear old lady. She had ideas that were worlds apart from her own. "Dan doesn't see me as a prospect. I'm certain of that because I'm not even Amish."

"People convert."

"Do they?"

"It happens."

"I didn't realize that. I suppose I knew people could if they wanted to badly enough."

"Yes. It's a decision that's made with the heart and with the head. To become Amish, you must give up all of the worldly ways and commit your life to God. This life is only temporary—like a vapor. It'll be over before we know it and then we have eternity with God if we acknowledge Him and do what He wants us to do while we're here." Ruth put her hand on Bridget's arm. "I'm sorry to prattle on. You must think I'm just a silly old fool."

"No, I don't. Not at all." Bridget swallowed hard. "Don't worry about me; I'll be okay. And Dan is not thinking of me as he would think of an Amish woman so don't worry about that. In fact, I've seen him with an Amish woman a couple of times."

"Is that right?"

"Yes. I'm certain she likes him."

"Many women like him. That's not my concern. Do you know he's the oldest Amish man in the community who's not married? Well, besides Samuel Esh, and Jacob Yoder, but they don't really count because—let's just say they'll probably never marry. My point is that Dan doesn't seem interested in any of the women about or any of the visiting women from other communities that I've introduced him to."

"Isn't it better that way?"

Ruth squinted as she stared at her. "What way is that?"

"Isn't it better that he makes a wise choice and is careful who he chooses since it's so important to make the right decision?"

"That's just it. I'm starting to think that he won't like anyone. There's been nothing wrong with the women I've introduced him to."

"You're quite close to him?"

"He's my nephew."

"Oh, I didn't realize."

"He lived with us for a while. His parents died. His mother when he was younger and then his father when he was fifteen. That's when he came and lived with us. His siblings were split up and taken in by other relations. It worked out well because one of my sons was close to his age."

Bridget thought back to Dan's story about the rocking horses. He'd said his father was good with doing woodwork. That must've been a memory he treasured and the reason why he gravitated toward working with wood.

Ruth continued, "Dan was only with us for a few years before he insisted on living by himself. He's very independent. There's been talk about him being seen with a young *Englisch* woman. Now, I shouldn't have told you that, but I'm worried that all isn't well with him. Anyway, you don't need to listen to my prattle."

"Do you want me to cancel dinner?" Bridget offered.

"No, no. I'm just concerned that's all. I don't want Dan to be swayed and you'd now be feeling vulnerable and needing a husband. As long as you know that Dan… well, he wouldn't be able to stay in the community if he married you. And I still don't know why he's been seen with a pretty young *Englisch* girl."

Bridget nodded and tried to keep the smile off her face. The Amish seemed to be purely black and white about relationships. "Don't men and women in your community have friendships?"

"They do. I just wanted to let you know where things stood."

"I don't feel that way about him, but thank you for the warning. I haven't had one thought about needing a husband since my husband has only just died."

Ruth nodded, and then turned around and walked back to her house.

Bridget turned and headed to the cabin hoping she hadn't been too harsh on Ruth. Anyway, now she knew she couldn't have a close friendship with Dan. She knew a little about the Amish and she already knew that they'd have to leave their faith if they married an outsider.

Dan was a handsome man and Bridget thought that maybe the young *Englisch* woman had found him attractive and had flirted with him—perhaps that's all that people had seen.

CHAPTER 10

This is my commandment, That ye love one another,
as I have loved you.
John 15:12

OVER DINNER in the restaurant that night, Dan said, "Ruth seems fond of you."

"Do you think so?"

"Yes. She's normally friendly, but she's never had people in her house when they stay in the cabin."

"I didn't know that." She hoped that Ruth and she would still be friends even though Ruth didn't like the idea of her going to dinner with Dan. "Ruth told me you used to live with her."

He nodded, as he'd just put a mouthful of food in his mouth. "I did," he eventually said. "Many years ago now. They took me in when my father died. My mother had already died some years before him."

"I guess Ruth and Jakob are like your second family, then."

"That's right. Ruth tends to be a worrier."

"I kind of noticed that."

He raised his eyebrows. "How so?"

Bridget shook her head and gave a small shrug of her shoulders not wanting to tattletale on Ruth.

"Did she tell you I'm taking too long to find a wife?"

"She didn't use those exact words, but she said something along those lines. I told her we were having dinner together and she thought… I'm not sure what she thought, but she didn't look happy."

Dan laughed. "She keeps telling me I'm the oldest bachelor around."

"It must be nice to have someone who cares so much about you."

"Don't you have that?"

"Dad plays golf nearly every day, even when it's raining, and Mom either goes to Bingo or watches TV. They care, but they've done their job of raising me and now I'm out of the nest and flying on my own."

"And are you close to your late husband's parents?"

"Not really. When we were in college, his parents divorced and his mother moved away and now she's married to someone else. His father just got married recently and he still lives in the family home. I should get back in touch with them soon. I haven't spoken to them since the funeral."

"You went to college with your husband?"

"We went to the same schools since we were nine. And we dated in college." Bridget spared him the whole story of how they'd gone from just friends to dating.

"That's nice. It must have been comforting to marry someone you'd known for a long time."

"It was." Bridget looked at him and saw him staring over her shoulder. She turned to see what he was staring at. It was a young woman of around eighteen years of age walking toward them.

He stood up. "Excuse me, Bridget."

He strode toward the young woman and Bridget stared after him.

"Who's she?" the young woman asked as Dan took her by the arm and led her outside.

Bridget turned to the front, figuring Dan might not be the genuine man he seemed. Dan was supposed to only have relationships with Amish women and she could tell that this young woman was jealous, and not only that, she was far too young for him.

A few minutes later, he sat back down, looking flushed in the face.

"A friend?" Bridget knew that had to be the young woman Ruth had concerns about.

He shook his head. "Someone I met recently."

After some silence, Bridget eventually asked, "Can I

ask why you've never married? It seems like in the Amish community people get married quite young."

He gave a quick raise of his eyebrows. "They do. I guess I was a late bloomer. Now I've got all kinds of people trying to match me with women who are either far too young for me or who are…"

"Desperate? Unsuitable?"

"Something like that. Well, maybe both of those things."

Bridget guessed he meant there were only the women who'd been passed over, but he was too polite to say so. "It's okay not to marry, isn't it?"

"It's acceptable; it's just a little unusual. Our lifestyle is based around the family and I'm not part of one, except the broader community which is a family in itself."

"I can see how that would make you feel."

"I keep busy."

"With making horses?" *Or with that young woman who was just here?* she wondered.

He smiled and nodded. "Sometimes I sleep in the workshop when I'm toiling long hours trying to get orders filled. Christmas is my busiest time."

She could tell that he'd much rather have a family than keep himself distracted by putting so many hours into his business.

"Have you ever lived outside of the Amish?"

"Only when I went on *rumspringa*. I felt lost when my father died. That's the only way I can explain it—

lost or on my own. I questioned everything and tried everything when I was living as an *Englischer.*" He chuckled.

"And yet you returned to the Amish. Do you find it hard to live with so many restrictions in what you can and can't do? I know a little bit about the Amish and it seems a harsh way of life."

"There's a reason for things that you see as restrictions. Are you talking about having no electricity?"

"Well, I guess that's the obvious one, and the horse and buggies. It's like stepping back in time."

"Hard work is what we're used to. With electricity would come things that would pull us away from *Gott.* The young ones like their TVs and their video games, which introduce things into their minds that aren't good. Even your newspapers are filled with disasters and strife."

"I understand that, but wouldn't it be so much easier if women had washing machines and dryers at least?"

"Some have gas-powered machines, and nothing replaces the sun for drying."

She couldn't keep the smile from her face.

He leaned forward. "Have I said something funny?"

"No. It's just that you seem to have an answer for everything. Now, what about the buggies?"

He laughed. "We like horses."

She laughed along with him.

He added, "The real reason is it's slowing the pace

of life and keeping us close to each other geographically."

"That makes sense."

"How long were you married, if you don't mind me asking?"

"Are you trying to change the subject?" she asked.

"You've learned a little about me; now I'd like to know more about you."

He was genuinely interested in her as a person. Now she could see the sense in what Ruth had said. The mood had switched from dinner with a friend to something that resembled a first date.

"I was married for ten years."

"That must be a hard adjustment for you to make."

"I'm taking it day-by-day."

When they finished the main meal, he asked. "Would you like dessert?"

"Not for me." She didn't want to keep the dinner going too long. The last thing she needed was a romantic entanglement and besides that, she was uneasy with the appearance of the young woman that Ruth had spoken of.

CHAPTER 11

If we confess our sins, he is faithful and just to forgive us our sins,
and to cleanse us from all unrighteousness.
1 John 1:9

BRIDGET SAID goodbye to Dan outside the restaurant. She could tell by the way he looked at her when they parted that he was interested in her as a woman. Ruth had been right to be concerned.

On the drive back to her cabin, she wondered if she should keep away from him. The last thing she wanted was to get her heart broken again. There were one hundred and one reasons why a relationship with an Amish man wouldn't work. For one, she wasn't about to convert to the Amish and it wasn't fair to pull someone away from their faith. She'd never be able to wear the old fashioned clothes and live an old fashioned life cut off from society. She drove past Ruth's house and parked her car near the cabin. Ruth would be keeping tabs on what time she arrived home, Bridget was certain of that.

AFTER HER CUP of tea the next morning, Bridget went for her usual walk before breakfast and saw Ruth digging about in the vegetable patch. "Good morning."

"Good morning. It's a lovely day, isn't it?"

"It certainly is."

"How was your dinner last night?"

Bridget was a little taken back that she asked that question so pointedly and so quickly. "Dinner was fine. There's really nothing to worry about. I'm not after a husband and he wouldn't be interested in me anyway." Bridget forced a giggle to make light of the situation.

Ruth dropped her gardening fork and stood up. "That's where you're wrong, Bridget. You are exactly the kind of strong woman that he would see himself with. And don't forget, I know him because I raised him from the time he was fifteen. He lived in my house. I know him better than anybody knows him."

"I've just lost my husband and the last thing I'm thinking…"

"Yes, we had this conversation yesterday. You

mightn't want a husband now, but you'll change your thinking as the baby grows in your belly."

Bridget shook her head. "I'm an *Englischer* and he's an Amish man. You're worried about nothing." Bridget wondered if she'd have to move on again and find somewhere else to stay until her house sold. Or, perhaps just move back to her house. "I'll keep walking."

CHAPTER 12

"Do not be afraid. Do not be discouraged,
for the Lord your God will be with you wherever you go."
Joshua 1:9

IF SHE HADN'T GIVEN her word to Dan that she would help him with the website, she would've abandoned the whole thing. Anyway, she'd already paid Ruth three months accommodation, so she had to stay put. With the baby coming, she had to watch every cent —she couldn't leave the cabin and be frivolous. Neither would it be right to ask for a refund to move on.

After giving careful consideration, Bridget decided the best thing she could do was tell Dan about her situation. He wouldn't be interested in her if he knew she was pregnant. She would wait for a good time to tell him

DAN AND BRIDGET had agreed to look for sites that would be good backdrops for the photographs of the rocking horses. The photographer said it would save money if they found the sites. He'd already described the backgrounds he wanted for the horses.

Dan pulled up in his buggy at eleven o'clock as he'd arranged. Once she heard him approach, she walked out the door closing the cabin door behind her. He jumped down and walked toward her.

"Please tell me you're coming with me in the car? I didn't stop to think about the buggy."

He laughed. "It will speed things up if we go in the car and I don't want to take up all your time. Give me a moment." He turned around, led his horse and buggy to Ruth's barn, and came back after a few minutes.

"Have you ever driven a car?" she asked while walking to the car.

"On *rumspringa,* I did."

After she clicked the car unlocked, they both got in.

"Go left when you get out of the driveway. We're heading to the Wilsons' farm. They've got a big red barn and I think there would be some other good backgrounds there."

"Good."

They traveled for a while in silence. She wasn't sure what to say to him.

"I had a nice time at dinner last night," she eventually said.

"Yes, it was good. What did Ruth say about you having dinner with me?"

She laughed. "What made you think I would've told her anything?"

"There was no reason not to. You mentioned that you see her every morning."

"Okay. If you must know, she is worried that you might be interested in me as more than a friend."

He laughed.

"I'm sorry to put you in a position like that," she said.

"It wasn't you. You haven't done anything. I should've been more careful and should never have asked you to dinner. It probably wasn't the right thing to do since you're staying here at the cabin."

"But it would've been alright if I wasn't staying at the cabin?"

"Maybe," he said with a hint of a smile.

She set her eyes back on the road. "It so beautiful out here. I don't know how I'm going to handle going back to a bigger town."

"Don't go. Stay close to here. It's a good place to live."

"I have to sell my house first. And it's not going well according to my realtor. The market's still in a slump and not looking like it's going to change any time soon." Bridget sighed. "If I did live around here, I suppose it'd be good to be close to my parents because they're getting older, but I don't want to be too close if you know what I mean. This might be a good distance away."

"Why would you want to live away from them?"

"Oh, I'm sorry!" Bridget remembered that his parents were gone and Amish were close with their families. "I'm sorry. It was a silly thing for me to say."

"Not at all; don't be sorry. You don't have to watch what you say around me. Just be yourself."

She wondered if now was the time to tell him. "I'm pregnant," she blurted out.

"You are?"

She glanced over at him. "I am. I just found out for sure in the last couple of days."

"That's wonderful news."

"Any other time it would be, but with Mattie gone…"

"It must be a hard time for you in that regard."

"I just have to carry on the best I can, and I guess I'm doing okay."

"You're a strong woman."

"I'm not at all. I've got no choice but to carry on. If I had a choice, I wouldn't be in this position with my husband gone."

"Will your parents help?"

"I doubt it. I shouldn't have told you, but I don't have a lot of people to speak with."

"I'm glad you told me."

She hoped she'd said enough to deter him from possibly thinking of her as a marital prospect ... if he'd been thinking of her in that way at all.

"Turn left here and then the first place on the right is the Wilsons' farm."

He directed her to pull the car up at the barn.

"I've written a list. I've got eleven different styles of rocking horses—we'll need eleven different backgrounds."

"So the Wilsons will let us wander around and choose some areas?"

"Yes. They'll be out in the fields and they said we could do what we want."

"Sounds good. I can take different photos with my phone and then we can look at them and see what we think about them."

"Good idea, and then we can go back to the store and think about it there. Have you got the time today to do all that?"

"I've got all the time in the world at the moment."

He smiled at her.

"Who's looking after the store today?"

"A good friend of mine is looking after it. You met her the other day."

"Oh yes, Deirdre. Does she do work for you often?"

"No. I told her what we were doing and she offered to look after the store."

"That was good of her."

"Yes, it was."

Bridget glanced up at him and wondered if he knew that the woman was interested in him romantically. Was he a typical male and blind to those kinds of things? And what about the pretty young *Englisch* woman? She was clearly jealous the other night. Bridget told herself whatever Dan was doing in his personal life was none of her business.

They spent the next two hours taking photos of suitable backgrounds.

"Would you like me to be with the photographer when he does his shoot?"

"I would love that. You do seem to have a flair for this kind of thing."

She laughed. "How would you know that?"

"I can just tell."

THEY GOT in the car to head back to the cabin.

Dan asked, "I've worked up quite an appetite. How about we stop and have lunch somewhere? There's a diner close to here; it's nothing fancy but the food's good."

She rubbed her neck, not sure whether she should be spending so much time with him outside of the project they had going. "I'm a little tired."

"Of course. I don't want to wear you out. Are you still coming into the store so we can look through the photos?"

"Can we do that first thing tomorrow? I'm a little tired. I could come to the store in the morning."

"Yes. That would be fine. Thank you for coming with me today."

When they got back to the cabin, he said goodbye and headed to his horse and buggy.

After Bridget had got inside the cabin, she stood close to the kitchen window and watched him leave. Even though she wanted to spend time with him, she was wary.

CHAPTER 13

Yea, though I walk through the valley of the shadow of death,
I will fear no evil: for thou art with me;
thy rod and thy staff they comfort me.
Psalm 23:4

MAX YOWLING woke Bridget the next morning. She sat up in bed and looked at him sitting on the floor by the bed. "What's wrong?"

He walked closer to her and then yowled again. It was his hungry meow. She got up and went over to his food bowl. He'd eaten all his dry food. Normally she left the dry food filled for him to graze on throughout the day and gave him his wet food at night.

"Are you hungry again?"

Once she shook some dry food into his bowl, he

pushed the pellets around with his nose and then ate some.

"I'm going back to sleep." When she was back in bed, she picked up her mobile phone to check the time. It was eight o'clock. That was the time she had been waking up since she'd been at the cabin. There was no use trying to get more sleep, as she'd told Dan she'd be at his store bright and early.

After she showered and changed, she headed off for her morning walk figuring that she'd buy breakfast along the way to Dan's.

"Morning, Bridget."

Bridget looked over at Ruth who was hanging sheets on her clothesline by her house. "Need a hand?"

"No, I'm fine thank you."

After she had given her a wave, Bridget kept walking hoping the grass, still wet from an early morning rain, wouldn't seep through her walking shoes and make her socks wet. It disturbed her that she kept thinking about Dan and was looking forward to seeing him. A fantasy was what it was. He represented the perfect man—honest, hard-working, and handsome in a rugged kind of way. The only down side to him was whatever he had going on with the young woman who had interrupted their meal.

None of that is any of my business, she reminded herself.

After her walk, she went back to the cabin and changed her shoes leaving on her track pants and t-shirt. Part of her wanted to look her best, but the more sensible side of her took over and she left the house looking plain and ordinary in very casual clothes.

WHEN SHE GOT to the store, she looked in the window to see him sweeping the floor.

"Doing some housekeeping?" she asked when she stepped in the door.

"All the time." He put on a funny voice. "'It never ends.' That was my impression of Ruth," he explained.

Bridget laughed. "I won't tell her you did that just now."

"No. Please don't! She wouldn't see the humorous side to it." He glanced at the broom. "I'll do this later."

"You can keep sweeping. I just called in to see if you wanted some coffee or something to eat? I left home without eating."

He shook his head. "Hasn't Ruth told you that breakfast is the most important meal of the day?"

"According to Ruth, every meal is the most important."

"That's true. I'm fine thanks."

"Are you sure? I'll feel bad if I'm having something and you're not," she explained.

"Okay. I could have a coffee."

"Good. I'll be right back." She placed her laptop on a bench.

Bridget returned with coffee for Dan and an egg and

bacon sandwich for herself. As she passed him the coffee, she said, "I didn't even ask if I could eat in here."

"Of course you can."

She followed him through to the workshop where he pulled up a chair for her so she could eat at a table.

"Thank you. Do you want to help me out with some of this?" With her hands wrapped around half the sandwich, she nodded to the other half.

He shook his head. "I've just eaten. It looks good, though. Don't hurry. Take your time. I've got a few accounts to look at while you eat."

While she was eating, customers came and went. He sold smaller rocking horses as ornaments, or possibly for smaller toys. Whatever people used them for, he turned over quite a few. She finished her sandwich and wiped her hands on a paper napkin. It was nice to eat something that she didn't have to cook.

"Finished?" he asked coming back into the workshop.

She nodded. "You seem to sell a lot of the smaller rocking horses."

"They're my bread and butter, so to speak, the ones that I sell to tourists. My larger rocking horse sales are the cream."

"Do you see much of your family—your brothers and sisters?"

He laughed. "How did we go from rocking horses to my brothers and sisters?"

She shrugged. "I'm sorry. I'm too nosey. I was thinking of you doing all this work on your own and I wondered if any of them helped you."

"We're all spread out now. I only have a brother who stayed close by. He has an apple orchard amongst other things and he's too busy to help me. He'd think I should help him. When I get busy, I've got plenty of people I can find to help me. We Amish are very good with our hands."

She took hold of her laptop and ran the photos from her phone through to the larger screen of her computer. He looked over her shoulder and was so close that she was nervous. "Here, you sit down in front of the screen." She jumped up and they exchanged places.

They discussed which background looked better for each of his different styles of rocking horses.

Once Bridget had it all jotted down, she closed the lid of her laptop. "That didn't take too long."

"Thanks once again, Bridget."

She shook her head. "Stop thanking me. You're making me nervous."

He laughed. "You seem a bit jittery today. Is everything alright?"

"As good as I can be under the circumstances."

"Let me know if I can be of any help—with anything. And, I mean that. I'm not just saying that to be polite."

"I don't think there'll be anything you can do, but I appreciate the offer."

"You're not going now, are you?"

Bridget laughed. "I've got things to do. I can't hang around here all day."

"I could give you things to do."

She shook her head. "I probably won't see you now until the photo shoot."

"Not unless you agree to have dinner with me again."

Without being able to keep the smile from her face, she said, "I can't."

He nodded and then he walked her to the front of the shop where they said goodbye.

CHAPTER 14

Trust in the Lord with all thine heart;
and lean not unto thine own understanding.
In all thy ways acknowledge Him and He shall direct thy paths.
Proverbs 3: 5-6

THE DAY of the photo shoot arrived, and Dan had arranged a truck to collect the rocking horses and take them to the Wilsons' farm. Dan had arranged for his friend, Deirdre, to stay back and look after his store while he and Bridget, and the photographer's intern, Brian, helped arrange the horses in the places Dan and Bridget had chosen.

WHEN THE PHOTO shoot was over, Bridget drove

back to the cabin alone. She opened the door, wishing she were going back to the store with Dan, but it would have been awkward with Deirdre there too.

"Hello, Max."

Max was asleep on the couch and didn't wake up when she spoke to him. She opened the fridge, made herself a sandwich and a cup of tea, and then she sat down next to Max. Bridget plonked her feet up on the coffee table and took a large bite of her sandwich.

She finally decided she had to spend more time with Dan, but she'd need a good excuse. That was when she thought she could do some work on his website and then she could show him what she'd done.

After lunch, she drove somewhere she could get Wifi and did some work on creating Dan's website. Part of her was saying she shouldn't become involved with an Amish man, but she didn't listen. What if he were her soul mate—the one she had been created for? If not, it sure felt nice that someone was paying her so much attention and being kind to her. That was what she needed right now.

She walked into his store two hours later with her laptop under her arm. Instead of Dan, Deirdre met her in the middle of the store.

"Hello, Deirdre." Bridget berated herself for not leaving things until the following day.

"Bridget, how are you?"

"I'm fine thank you. Is Dan in?"

"He's left me here to mind the store while he went

to get some supplies."

"Do you know how long he'll be?"

"I think he'll be quite some time. He normally takes a while when he goes to his suppliers."

"Did he only just leave?"

"Yes. He told me the photo shoot went well."

"It went really well. The photographer will be emailing the shots through to me in a couple of days after he's done his magic on them. Touching them up and things like that."

"I want to thank you for helping Dan with everything. He really didn't know where to go with this website. He says you've been a huge and really needed help to him."

The woman was speaking as though she and Dan were closer than he'd let on. Bridget knew Dan wouldn't have misled her because she was sure that was not in his nature. Was this woman trying to subtly claim ownership of Dan in making out she was closer to him than she was? Either way, it was something that Bridget didn't want to get in the middle of. This woman had an obvious attraction to Dan and now it was loud and clear to Bridget she should leave Dan well and truly alone. Nothing could come of her attraction to him.

"I'm glad to be of help." Perhaps if she stayed and talked with Deirdre, Dan would arrive. No, she should go and go now! "You see, I'm on bit of a break away from work."

"That's nice and you're staying at Ruth's cabin?"

"That's right. It's such a lovely quiet place. I'm thinking I might buy a house around here when mine sells."

Deirdre nodded. "It is a nice area, I guess. I've lived here all my live and I don't know what it's like anywhere else."

"I should go. I just came in to tell Dan that I've done a little work on his website, but I can tell him later."

"I'll give him the message."

"Thank you, Deirdre." Bridget walked to her car, mad with herself for going to his store so soon.

"Bridget!"

She had just put her hand on her car door about to open it when she heard Dan's voice. She swung around. "Hello."

He hurried to her. "Are you leaving?"

"I am. I just came to tell you that I've done a little work on your website, but I can tell you about that later. I've got somewhere to be."

"I'm so glad. It's all thanks to you that this is finally coming about."

Bridget smiled. "I can barely wait to see the photos."

"Me too."

"Your bishop lets you have Internet and power in your store, I noticed."

"We're allowed modern technology for our businesses these days."

Bridget nodded. "That's good."

"You approve?"

She studied his face and a smirk was turning his lips slightly upward.

She laughed. "I do."

"Do you have to go? Why don't you come back to the store and tell me all about the work you've done?"

Bridget wouldn't feel comfortable with Deirdre there. "I should go."

"Come on. I'll get us some coffee from the café."

"Forget the coffee. I've lost the taste for it in the last few days. But I could go for one of their cakes."

"Done. You wait in the store and tell Deirdre I won't be long."

Dan hurried to the café and Bridget headed back to the store.

"Dan said that he was bringing us back some coffee and I should wait here," she told Deirdre.

"Is he bringing me one?"

"Yes. He wants to hear about the website."

"Is there much to tell?"

"Not really, just a bit. I guess Dan's excited to finally get one up and running soon."

Once Bridget was sitting on a chair in the workshop, Dan came back in with two cakes and one cup of coffee.

When he saw Deirdre, he smiled and passed her the coffee. "Here you go, Deirdre."

She smiled at him. *"Denke,* Dan."

Bridget was fairly certain that Dan had forgotten to get Deirdre a coffee and had given Deirdre his own.

He sat down along with them. "Have you been busy, Deirdre?"

Bridget noticed that now he had three chairs in the workshop where previously he'd only had one.

Deirdre answered, "I've had some sales and a lot of people looking. One lot said they'd come back and put an order in for Christmas. I didn't know how to do that, so they're coming back at four this afternoon."

"That's good," he said smiling back at her. "That'll make the day worthwhile. Now, what happened today, Bridget?" he asked while pulling two small cakes out of a white paper packet.

Bridget reached out and took one of the cakes. Before she took a bite, she told them what she had done with the website.

Deirdre listened, sitting close to Dan and laughing every so often.

As soon as Bridget finished the cake, she left the two of them alone.

Driving back to the cottage, she knew that Deirdre saw her as some kind of competition for Dan's interest and it wasn't fair to get in Deirdre's way. She wondered why Dan didn't seem attracted or at all interested in Deirdre—it was plain to see, but Deirdre didn't seem to notice. If he were interested, then surely they would've become a couple by now.

CHAPTER 15

The wicked, through the pride of his countenance,
will not seek after God: God is not in all his thoughts.
Psalm 10:4

BRIDGET HAD LEFT Dan's store not knowing when she'd hear from him again. When she got home, she made herself a cup of hot chamomile tea and settled down on the couch to read a book.

An hour into her book, there was a knock on her door. Expecting that it was Ruth come to check on how she was, she was surprised when she opened the door to see Deirdre.

"Deirdre! Do you want to come in?"

Deirdre nodded and stepped through the door. "I hope you don't mind me coming to see you. I was just about to visit Ruth and Jakob and thought I'd call in and see you too."

"That's nice." When Deirdre didn't say anything, she asked, "Is everything okay?"

"I've just come to ask you if Dan has said anything to you about me?"

"Like what?"

"Anything at all."

"He said you were looking after the store for him today." She shook her head. "Nothing apart from that. You appear to be good friends."

"Oh." She looked disappointed. "And that's all?"

"Yes, but we're not exactly friends. He wouldn't confide anything in me if that's what you might think."

"I'm sorry I came." She turned and hurried toward the door.

"You don't have to leave."

Deirdre spun around. "I just want to know what he's thinking, that's all. I thought he might have said something to you because you're an *Englischer* and he probably would've thought whatever he said to you wouldn't get around." Deirdre put a hand on the door and then immediately burst into tears.

"What's wrong?"

"It's Dan. I've waited for him for years and I don't know if I can wait any longer. There are rumors he's seeing an *Englischer* and then there's another man who wants to marry me. I want to marry Dan, but he hasn't asked me. I just don't know what to do."

All Bridget could do was pat her on the arm. "Love's so hard. I don't know what to tell you to do. I don't know what I'd do if I were in your position."

"I'm sorry. I shouldn't have come here, but I just need to know what he's thinking, that's why I asked you. Soon, if he doesn't ask to marry me, I'll have to marry Andrew."

"That must be a hard position to be in. And how do you feel about Andrew?"

"I like him as a good friend."

"Sometimes they're the best kind of people to marry. The man I married wasn't my first choice, but we were happy."

Deirdre stared at her. "You've been married?"

"Oh, I should've explained. My husband was killed recently. I'm now on my own."

"You're a widow?"

"Yes, that's what I am, I guess. I never really gave it too much thought that I would ever be in this position, but anyway back to you. Mattie and I were happy and, as I said, he wasn't my first choice."

"I thought you might be interested in Dan." Deirdre looked at the floor and then looked back to Bridget. "I've been a fool. What happened to your first choice?"

"It's a long sordid story. I saw him recently and then I was glad I didn't marry him. He's not the man I once thought he was. My best friend was my best choice."

"Now you've made the decision very difficult for me."

Seeing a small smile on Deirdre's face, Bridget said, "I told you I wasn't the best person to speak to. I can barely run my own life."

The two women laughed.

"Why don't you ask Dan straight out how he feels?"

"I couldn't do that. What if he rejects me?"

"At least then you'll know."

"I suppose that's true, but that would be embarrassing and then what if Andrew learned of the conversation? Things have a way of getting around the community. Somehow, someway things always get around. Could you ask him for me?"

Bridget gasped. "No! I couldn't. I don't know him well enough and that's far too personal a thing to ask him."

"That's exactly why I need you to find out. He'll tell you what he really thinks."

"I couldn't. It's got nothing to do with me. That's awkward."

"Please, Bridget, please help me; as one woman to another."

Bridget shook her head. "No, I can't. Not if you're basing the rest of your life on information I give you. I can't be responsible for that. Believe me, it's best that you speak to him yourself and take the risk that Andrew will find out. I don't see how he would because Dan wouldn't say anything to anybody. I get the idea Dan's not that kind of a man."

"That might be what you do because you're an *Englischer,* but our lifestyle and culture are different."

"But it's just honesty, isn't it?"

Deirdre pulled a face. "I suppose you're right."

"You could pray about it and then see what you feel led to do."

"That's a good idea. I've prayed about it before, but I'll pray about it again. See? You are good at this."

Bridget laughed. "Can I get you a cup of hot tea or a coffee?"

"Thank you, but another time? I really should be going. My sisters have a roadside stall and I help them pack every evening."

"Come over any time. I'm mostly here."

"Thank you, Bridget."

Bridget desperately wanted to know who this young woman was that Dan had been seen with, but managed to stop herself from asking. Instead, Bridget stood still in the doorway and watched Deirdre walk to Ruth's house. She was glad she wasn't in a situation like Deirdre. She remembered what it was like going through the emotional ups and downs of liking someone and them not feeling the same, and also being in love and ending up with nothing but a broken heart.

CHAPTER 16

And he said, Blessed be thou of the LORD, my daughter: for thou hast shewed more kindness in the latter end than at the beginning, inasmuch as thou followedst not young men, whether poor or rich.
Ruth 3:10

IT WAS two days later when she saw Dan again. It was late in the evening when Bridget heard a buggy and she looked out the window, secretly hoping that it might be Dan.

When she opened the door, she was pleased to see that it was he, and he was heading to her place and not to Ruth's house

When he looked up and caught her eye, he smiled.

At that moment, she knew she was in trouble. She'd only had those pangs in her stomach once before.

"I just thought I would let you know that Peter emailed the photos to me and they're brilliant, each and everyone of them. I was hoping you would have come into the shop so you could've seen them."

"I wasn't sure when he'd be sending them through. I thought he said he'd email them to me, anyway, it's fantastic that you like them."

"Why don't you come back to the store with me now? We can look at them together. I'd appreciate knowing what you think about them. After that, I can take you for a bite of dinner somewhere."

"Well I… ar…"

"I don't smell dinner cooking," he said with a cheeky grin.

She smiled. "I didn't realize what time it was. I was engrossed in my book."

"I'll let you drive me if you don't want to take the buggy." He raised his eyebrows and leaned forward waiting for an answer.

"I'll accept your kind invitation, especially since we don't have to go in the buggy."

He laughed. "I'll get you into the buggy one day."

"I don't know about that," she said. "I'll just shut some windows."

"Don't worry about that. It's not going to rain. No one will steal anything around these parts. Besides, they'd have to get past Ruth first." He laughed.

"I'm not used to that. I'm used to locking doors and windows."

"Well, you don't have to here."

"I'll get my bag." She stopped by the bathroom, fixed her hair and put on some lipstick.

"I got an email from the person you arranged to set up the website. It's all ready to go. You just need to show me how to enter the information and the images. He said it's easy so I should be able to operate it for myself once I know how."

"That's right. I'll show you what to do and it *is* easy."

"I'm not used to websites and things like that; it took me a long time to figure out how to send an email."

"It won't take long. You just need to be shown what to do and then do it a couple of times yourself and then you'll be set."

"That's what I'm hoping. I don't mean for you to show me everything today, I still haven't worked out what I want to say about each one. I just want to show you the images tonight."

"That's good, because that's all you'll be getting. I run out of steam towards the end of the day."

WHEN BRIDGET SAT down at the table in his shop, he moved some things away from his computer. Out of the paperwork fell a photograph of a blonde-haired woman. Dan immediately snapped it up off the floor and pushed it back into the paperwork.

Certain it was the mysterious young woman, Bridget asked, "I thought Amish didn't believe in taking photographs of themselves?"

"That woman isn't Amish. It's a long story."

"Do you want to tell me about it?"

He laughed. "It's best left for another day." He sat down next to her and brought up his emails and flipped through them until he found Peter's emails that contained the images.

The images were as good as Dan had said, but Bridget's mind was still on Dan's mystery woman.

WHEN BRIDGET LAY in bed that night, she was pleased she'd refused Dan's dinner invitation. She knew how this would end between them if she dared to cross the invisible line between their two cultures. Reminding herself that he was Amish and she was not, she also had the added disturbance of the mystery woman. She'd been heartbroken once by a man choosing another woman over her and she was not about to risk it again.

Bridget knew if she stayed any longer, she'd fall hopelessly in love with Dan.

CHAPTER 17

Know therefore that the LORD thy God, he is God, the faithful
God, which keepeth covenant and mercy with them that love
him and keep his commandments to a thousand generations;
Deuteronomy 7:9

As soon as the light was over the horizon the next morning, Bridget packed her car and scribbled off a note to Ruth explaining she'd left and wasn't coming back. She figured Ruth would see her gone, and in a few days time she would walk into the cabin and find the note. She couldn't go through with a goodbye and answering any questions that Ruth and Jakob might ask about where she was going and why.

With Max in the cat-carrier in the backseat and all her possessions in the car, she headed back to her parents' house. She'd stay with them until her house sold, and very soon, she'd have to tell them they were about to become grandparents.

"WHAT ARE you doing back here? Do you know Max can't stay in the house?"

That had been the greeting from her mother.

Bridget walked past her mother. "I was just walking through to the laundry room."

When Max was settled, she came out into the living room just as her father came through the front door.

"Come here!" Her father was in the kitchen and walked toward her.

Bridget walked into his arms and he enclosed her in a warm hug. At least her father was pleased to see her.

"How long will you be staying here?" her mother asked.

Her father butted in, "Bridget can stay here as long as she likes; she doesn't have to give us the time. She can come and go as she pleases."

"It's easy for you to say because you don't do any of the cleaning, all the cooking, or have to organize any of the meals or the washing."

"Sit down, Dad. I have something to tell you both."

He glanced at his watch. "Will it take long? I'm due at a game soon."

"Have you won the lottery, or have you sold your house?" her mother asked.

"It's nothing like that." When they were all seated, Bridget took a deep breath, and said, "I am going to have a baby."

Her mother looked at her father, who seemed to be pleased.

"We are going to be grandparents," he said.

"Whose is it?" her mother asked.

"The baby's Mattie's, of course. What are you talking about, Mom?"

"And you're only finding out about it now?"

"I've known for a few weeks, but I just wanted to come back here and tell you in person."

"I'm very happy for you, then, if this is what you want."

"Of course this is what she wants, dear," her father said.

"Well, I'm very happy. Although, I'm not quite sure if I'm old enough to be a grandmother."

"Yes, you are and that's what you will be. You better get used to it and figure out what you want to be called —granny, nanna, or whatever it is you want. You too, Dad."

Her father chuckled.

"Is it a boy or a girl?" her mother asked.

"They didn't tell me and I don't want to know. Boy or a girl, it doesn't matter to me."

"Nat will be pleased to see you; he's been hounding us for your address. I don't think he believes that we didn't know where you're staying."

So much had happened she forgot one of the reasons she had left was Nat.

"I'll stay on here for a while if that's okay." She looked at both parents who nodded. "Are you happy?" she asked them.

"We are if you are." Her mother looked at her anxiously.

"I'm fine, Mom."

"We could turn one of the spare rooms into a nursery. If you want to stay on here for good, it'll be much easier if you stay with us."

"Thanks, Mom, but I'll buy something when my house sells. Thanks for the offer."

"You can come here whenever you like. Don't forget that."

"You won't live far away from us will you?" her father asked.

Her mother gasped. "You won't move back to Oklahoma, will you?"

"No. We were only there for his job."

"That's good. I'd like to keep you close by," her father said.

THAT NIGHT, she just stepped out of the shower when her mother knocked on the door.

"Nat's here to see you. He's sitting in the living room. Hurry up. You've been in there for a long time."

"Okay but I have to get dressed."

"Well, hurry up."

When she walked out and saw Nat, she felt nothing, nothing at all. If only she had felt nothing all those years ago; then things would've been a lot easier for her.

Nat walked over and kissed her on the cheek. "Are you home for good?"

"I'm not sure."

"Hope you'll stay. Your parents said you have some news?"

She glared at her mother who was sitting across at the other side of the living room and her mother looked away. Her father had already made an escape to his bedroom for an early night.

"I'm pregnant."

"You are? That's great news. Congratulations."

"Thank you. I found out a couple of weeks ago. It was a bit of a surprise, but I guess these things happen."

"Yes, we even talked about that, neither of us having any children, but now you will. When is the baby due?"

"July. The beginning of July."

He nodded. "Well, that is good news. Why don't you come out for a drink with me and we'll celebrate?"

"I can't drink; I'm pregnant."

"Come out with me and watch me drink, then."

Bridget laughed. "Are you thinking tonight?"

"There's no time like the present."

Bridget shook her head. "No. I couldn't possibly. I'm too tired after driving here today."

"Where were you exactly?"

"I'll tell you later." It was a delaying tactic. She had no intention of telling him where she had been in case she went back there one day. He would probably follow her there. She yawned and did nothing to cover it up hoping Nat would take the hint and leave.

"Can I see you tomorrow?" he asked.

"I'll be busy all day tomorrow."

"What about tomorrow night?"

"No. I have been getting very tired."

He didn't stop there. "What about lunch the day after tomorrow?"

"Maybe if I don't have an appointment that I might have forgotten about. You see, I'm trying to get in to see a doctor who's been recommended to me."

"Okay. You look a bit tired. I'll leave you alone." He stood up, leaned over and kissed her on the cheek. "I'll see you soon."

She walked him to the door and was pleased when she closed the door behind him. She wondered what she'd ever seen in him.

"You could do worse, you know," her mother said.

Bridget stared at her mother wondering if she'd been speaking to herself. "What do you mean?"

"You know what I mean. Nat's in love with you and you need a husband. Think of your child. It's not going to be easy doing it all yourself. People might think you just got pregnant and never had a husband."

"They can think what they want. I had a husband and he's gone now and that's all I can think about. It's not like Mattie was a goldfish that I can just go out and replace." Bridget walked past her mother and hurried to the safety of her bedroom. Maybe it had been a mistake coming back. Now she didn't feel as though she was at home anywhere.

"No need to be like that. Just suck it up," she heard her mother call out to her before she closed her bedroom door.

All her life her mother had told her to 'suck it up,' which meant put on a happy face no matter what bad things were happening. Her mother and father never showed emotion and every time she had shown some as a child, she'd been shut down. 'Suck it up,' meant to keep her emotions hidden.

CHAPTER 18

Know therefore that the LORD thy God, he is God, the faithful
God, which keepeth covenant and mercy with them that love
him and keep his commandments to a thousand generations;
Deuteronomy 7:9

Now sitting on her blue bedspread, she stared at
the images of the pop stars in the posters on her wall.
There had to be a better life for her somewhere—
maybe with someone—one day. Closing her eyes, she
prayed that God would lead her to the life that was the
best for her and her unborn child. It no longer mattered
about her happiness so much. Now, it was about her
child and giving him or her the best life possible.

When she opened her eyes, her stomach churned.
How would she know which way God wanted her to

go? Would she see the signs that God would show her? If only she'd listened and been more attentive to God's ways years ago then maybe she would be in a better situation right now.

A sense of knowing suddenly flooded peace into her heart. All she had to do was wait and trust—she didn't have to plan out her entire life at this very moment. All she had to do was know that He would not let her down. One step at a time was all she had to take.

WHEN BRIDGET WOKE the next morning, she knew she couldn't stay with her parents, especially with her old boyfriend as close as the next-door house. After she dressed, she hurried down the stairs to find her father eating toast while reading the morning paper. Her mother was at the sink pouring herself a cup of coffee.

"Mom, Dad, I'm leaving today. I'm going back to the cabin."

"Why? It doesn't make any sense," her mother said.

"It makes sense to me. I like it there." She couldn't tell them she didn't feel at home there anymore because they'd be hurt.

"Will you give us the address at least?" her father asked.

"I will, but only if you promise not to give it to Nat."

"We won't."

She sat down at the kitchen table and scribbled out the address. "Now hide it," she said to her father.

"When are you leaving?" her mother asked

"As soon as I pack the car."

"It seems senseless. Why don't you stay a few more days?" her father asked. "Don't rush off like this."

"No. I want to get organized, and I'll have my baby in the hospital closest to the cabin. It's only about ten miles away. I've got a good doctor there and everything."

"Are you sure? We could redo your room and make another room for the baby," her mother suggested.

Bridget shook her head.

"Do you want some toast?" Her mother held up some bread.

"Yes, please."

Once her mother put the bread in the toaster, she turned around and stared at Bridget. "Who will look after you when the baby is born? I could come and stay in the cabin with you if you don't want to come back here."

"Thanks, Mom. I think I'll be okay. I'll call you from the hospital after the baby's born."

"I hope you'll call us before that," her father said.

"You can call me. You've got my cell number. Just don't give my number to Nat either."

"I'll give you a hand to pack the car before I go."

"That would be wonderful, thanks, Dad."

. . .

WHEN BRIDGET GOT BACK to the cabin, her note was lying on the table untouched. She heaved a sigh of relief that she could go back to normal and no one would know she had left.

The next time Bridget saw Ruth, she arranged to keep staying at the cabin for a longer period of time. She'd tossed between going back home to have her baby or staying put, and staying put won. Where else could she go? She couldn't go back to her parents while Nat was still living next door.

CHAPTER 19

Fulfil ye my joy, that ye be likeminded, having the same love,
being of one accord, of one mind.
Philippians 2:2

BRIDGET SAT in bed just hours after giving birth. She'd had a couple of hours sleep and that was all. It was morning, the beginning of the first day of her child's life. The baby was a girl, just a little over eight pounds. All had gone well, and Bridget still had twinges of pain across her lower abdomen and soreness in other places, which the nurse assured her were all very normal.

She stared down at the small baby girl in her arms and knew that all of her life, everything that had happened to her in the past, had led to this moment. If

Nat hadn't broken her heart, leading her to rebound and marry Mattie, she wouldn't be sitting here holding her beautiful baby girl. The baby was a gift from God and Mattie had to be looking down watching both of them. She was perfect in every way and Bridget could not keep her eyes from her miracle baby—her gift from God.

With tears in her eyes, she whispered, "I'll look after our baby girl well, Mattie."

While doing her prenatal course, Bridget had made two friends who lived close by, and friends were something she hadn't had for some time. They'd already had their babies earlier that week and had only just gone home from the hospital. Bridget felt good about having friends to visit who had babies the same age, especially since her baby would be an only child.

She looked up when she saw people come into the room. It was her parents. Her father had a bunch of pink roses and they were both grinning from ear-to-ear.

With her baby still in her arms, she tried to push herself further up her bed.

"Stay there, don't move," her mother said. "Can I hold her?"

"Of course you can, but the nurses insist on clean hands."

Her mother went to the sink and washed her hands, and then carefully took the baby from her and showed her to Bridget's father.

"She's so precious." Her father leaned forward and kissed Bridget's forehead.

"Are you sure you don't want to come home, Bridget? I'll even let Max in the house. He doesn't have to stay in the laundry room," her mother said.

Bridget laughed. Her parents weren't so bad after all. "I'll see how it goes, Mom. Thanks for the offer."

"Our place is your place. You can come and go as you please," her father said.

"And you're okay, Bridget?" Her mother still stared at the baby.

"I'm fine. Everything went really well. The birth only lasted five hours. I'm told that's good for a first one."

"Goodness! You're not thinking of having any more, are you?" her mother asked.

"No, Mom, relax! I'm just repeating what they told me. I'm not planning anything."

Soon after her parents left, Ruth peeped into her room.

"Are you up for visitors?"

"Hi Ruth, come in."

Ruth walked into the room, glanced at the baby who was now asleep in her small hospital crib beside the main bed. "I have Jakob and Dan here too. They'd like to see you."

Bridget looked down at herself to make sure she was decent and then covered herself further with a hand knitted shawl that she'd picked up days ago from a local Amish market. "Sure, I'd like to see them."

Ruth walked back to the door and gave them the okay to come into the room. They all milled around looking at the baby.

"Thank you all for coming," Bridget said.

They smiled, while Dan walked forward.

"Are you okay?" he asked.

"I'm good. Perfectly fine."

"I haven't seen you around lately. I'm happy things went well, and you've got a beautiful baby."

Bridget smiled at him. She didn't even care that she had no makeup on and her long fair hair was probably all over the place. They had a connection, which went beyond the shallow illusion of physical appearance. That's what she told herself, because at that moment, she wouldn't have had the strength to pretty herself up for visitors.

She could tell from the way Dan looked at her that he cared for her, and deeply.

"If she weren't asleep, I'd pick her up and cuddle her," Ruth said.

"There will be plenty of time for cuddles." Bridget laughed.

"When will you be ready to leave, Bridget?" Jakob asked.

"I'm not sure. I think I'll be here for a couple of days, at least."

"Dan or I could come and collect you," he offered.

"Yes, I'd be more than happy to do anything like that," Dan agreed.

"No, that's okay, thank you. I'll just get a taxi." She knew they'd have to go to the hospital by taxi and take her home by taxi since it was too far away for the buggies to travel.

"You'll let us know if you need anything, won't you?" Dan asked. "You can call me at the store."

She nodded. "I will."

A nurse came into the room to take Bridget's blood pressure, and her guests decided it was time to leave.

"You're not Amish, are you?" the nurse asked Bridget after her visitors had gone.

"No, I'm staying in a cabin on an Amish farm. They've been very good to me."

"They're good people. That younger man was quite good looking. Anything going on there?"

Bridget laughed. "That's the last thing on my mind."

"You're single, aren't you? It says so on your chart." The nurse's eyes were full of mischief.

"How's that blood pressure going?" Bridget asked.

"Yours is fine, but mine's slightly raised." The nurse fanned her face with her hand.

Bridget laughed again. "I could give you his phone number."

The nurse held up her hand to show a wedding ring. "Too late. Otherwise, I might consider taking you up on that." The nurse then turned her attention to the baby. "How's the feeding going?"

"I'm trying to get used to it. I don't think she's had much to drink. I'm a little worried."

"They don't need much in the first few days. The few drops they get are all they need until your milk comes in. When you're both handling feeding properly, then we'll let you go home."

"How will I know when my milk comes in?"

The nurse giggled. "Believe me you'll know."

CHAPTER 20

Finally, brethren, whatsoever things are true, whatsoever things are honest, whatsoever things are just, whatsoever things are pure, whatsoever things are lovely, whatsoever things are of good report; if there be any virtue, and if there be any praise, think on these things.
Philippians 4:8

BRIDGET WAS RELEASED from the hospital on day four after the baby was born. She stepped out of the taxi pleased to be back at the cabin. It wasn't her permanent home, but it was close enough to make her feel glad to be there.

The driver had brought her belongings into the cabin for her, and when the driver left her alone, she sat down, staring at the baby girl in her arms and wondering what to name her.

Ruth poked her head in the door. "Let me see her."

"Do you want to hold her?"

Ruth sat next to her. "There's nothing I'd like better."

Bridget carefully passed the baby over. "Now that you've got her, I'll unpack a few things if you don't mind."

"Not at all. I'll stay as long as you want me to."

"Thank you for looking after Max."

"It was no trouble."

Ruth sat and cooed at the baby while Bridget sorted out some washing that needed to be done. The baby's room had been prepared ahead of time with everything she'd need—clothes, diapers and plenty of towels and linen.

"Your phone's ringing," Ruth called out when Bridget was trying to get organized.

"Coming." Bridget headed back to the small living area and shook out her phone from her bag.

"Where have you been, Bridget?" the female voice on the other end of the line demanded.

"Having a baby. Who's this?"

"Oh, congratulations. It's Jenny. I've sold your house. I need you to sign some papers."

"You have?"

"I just need your signature."

"That's great news. Wait a minute. What price?"

"Asking price. They'd sold their house and they needed one in a hurry and yours suited them down to the ground."

"Full asking price?"

"Yes. It's unheard of in this market. You were lucky."

"Thank you."

"Can I fax the papers to you somewhere?"

"Yes. Just email them to me and I'll get them back to you tomorrow." Bridget ended the call and looked across at Ruth.

"You'll be leaving us soon?" Ruth asked.

"Yes. My house has been sold—finally."

"I'm happy for you." Ruth didn't look happy.

Bridget sat down with her. "I don't know what I would've done without you and Jakob, Ruth. You gave me a place that I could call home when I needed somewhere to stay. You've been a good friend."

Ruth looked down at the baby. "She's beautiful. Have you thought up a name yet? Oh, I don't want her to go. It was the best time in my life when I had small babies."

Bridget giggled. "We haven't gone yet. I'll need to find another house first. I'm hoping a name will come to me soon. I'll have to send papers off soon for her birth certificate."

"What are your family names?"

"My mother is... No! I want her to have a name that is just her own."

"Like what?"

Bridget giggled. "I'm having trouble thinking of one."

"What are some of your favorite names?"

"I've always liked the name Olivia."

"Why not call her Olivia? That's a beautiful name."

"Do you think so?'

"I do. Have your parents seen her yet?"

"Yes, they came to the hospital to see her just before you did. You might have even passed them in the hospital. I was a little surprised they visited because they didn't go to Mattie's funeral, but I guess that was too far for them to travel."

"Don't underestimate the bond that they're going to have with this little one."

"I guess I did, and maybe I might have misjudged them."

"It's an easy thing to do. So, Olivia?"

"Olivia Logan? Does it sound all right?" Bridget asked Ruth.

"It sounds perfect and look at her little face. She fits it so well."

Bridget looked down at her sleeping baby. She hadn't expected she would be so beautiful immediately after being born. Many newborns were wrinkled, but her baby was full faced and gorgeous. It might have been that she saw her baby as no one else did.

"We'll have to start looking for a house."

"Don't look too hard." Ruth chortled. "Will you stay close by?"

"I love it here. It feels like home. I won't go too far away."

"Good! And this little one will have to come back and visit her Aunt Ruth."

WHEN RUTH LEFT THE CABIN, it had been great timing because, before Ruth got back to her house, Dan pulled up in his buggy. Bridget watched from the window of her cabin with her sleeping baby in her arms to see that Dan and Ruth exchanged a quick greeting and a few words before Dan continued toward the cabin.

CHAPTER 21

Nevertheless let every one of you in particular so love his wife
even as himself;
and the wife see that she reverence her husband.
Ephesians 5:33

BY THE TIME Bridget got from her window to the doorway, Dan was right in front of her.

"Have you just got home?" he asked.

"Yes. Come inside."

He walked inside and stared at the baby. "I can't get over how tiny she is."

"Would you like to hold her now?"

"Could I?"

"Yes. Just mind her head." Bridget passed her over carefully.

"This feels a little odd."

"Let's sit down."

Once they were on the couch, Dan blinked a couple of times and she was sure he was trying to stop tears.

"I have something in my eye. Do you have a tissue or something?"

"Yes." Bridget jumped up and came back with a box of tissues.

He cradled the baby carefully in one arm while pulling out a tissue with his free hand. Dabbing at his right eye, he said, "I just had something in my eye."

Bridget sat quietly. It was nice to see a man getting emotional. He was nothing like her parents who buried their feelings.

He pushed the tissue into a top pocket of his work pants. "There's something I'd like to share with you, Bridget. I feel that we've become close enough for me to say this. And now with your daughter in my arms, it seems like this is the right time."

She inhaled deeply hoping he might propose to her.

"I have a daughter," he blurted out and then stared at her.

There were a million questions she wanted to ask but didn't want to overwhelm him. Where, who, why—how?

He continued, "No one in the community knows yet. I didn't know myself until recently."

"The young woman you've been seen with?" Bridget

considered he might be old enough to be her father if he'd had her at a young age.

His jaw dropped open. "I didn't know talk had gotten around."

"I'm afraid there has been talk."

He shook his head. "That's not good. I had hoped to keep it quiet for now. She's the young woman who interrupted us when we were having dinner together when you first came here. The reason I haven't told anyone is that Lacey is disturbed that I'm Amish and didn't marry her mother. I didn't know about her—that's why. I had a relationship with Lacey's mother while I was on *rumspringa,* and then I returned to the community and never heard from her again. Next thing I know, Lacey is knocking on my door."

"What did she say?"

"Her mother died recently and left her a letter explaining who I was. Apparently, she'd kept my identity secret from Lacey all her life."

"Poor Lacey. She grew up never knowing who her father was."

He shook his head. "I didn't know about her. If I had known, things would've been far different. I never would've left a woman to face that alone."

"What would you have done?"

"Whatever it took." Tears came to his eyes again.

"Thank you for telling me."

"I don't have anyone else in my life who'd understand."

"How are things between you and Lacey now?"

"Not good. Not good at all. She blames me for everything and can't understand why I left her mother. And when I say everything, I mean, everything."

"Teenagers are like that. How old is she?"

"She's just turned twenty."

"She'll come around. It's a difficult time for her with her mother dying and finally finding out who her father is."

"I hope so. I feel a connection with you. I feel like I can trust you."

"You can. You never thought to tell Deirdre?"

"No. Deirdre wants something that I can't give her and she doesn't need to hear my problems."

Bridget remained silent, not willing to ask what it was he couldn't give her—she guessed he meant that he couldn't give her his love.

He looked down at the baby in his arms. "This is a time for celebrating and I'm being a wet blanket. Forgive me."

"What I've found out is that babies bring out emotions in people. They soften people somehow."

"They do."

"Where do things stand between you and your daughter now?" She'd held her own child in her arms and she imagined that Dan would have been sad for the lost years with Lacey.

"It'll take time and I guess she's right to blame me.

I would've preferred her mother to ask me to stay and to have told me why I should've."

"Maybe she wanted you to choose her over the community without the child she was carrying weighing in as a factor."

"I've given it a lot of thought since my daughter showed up. I don't think Donna would've known she was pregnant when I left; if she had, it would've only been early days. But, I think you're right; she didn't want to influence my decision. I only wish she had. Lacey had a tough time of it without a father."

Bridget stared at her child and felt an overwhelming desire to protect her. "I hope my baby doesn't."

"I'm sorry. I shouldn't have said that. I'm sure your baby will have a good life. You'll see to that."

"I'll do everything in my power to see to it. It's funny that I never had a driving urge to be a mother, and now I can't imagine not having Olivia in my life."

"That's her name?"

Bridget nodded.

"It's a lovely name. I know what you mean about becoming a parent. When Lacey told me who she was, who her mother had been, it was the oddest feeling. This young woman was a stranger, and yet she was at the same time, well, she was a part of me."

"It must have been a shock."

"There are no words to describe the emotions that ran through me when she told me everything. I'm not an emotional man either." He looked down at the baby and then stared at Bridget. "What are your plans?"

"I forgot to tell you. I just found out today that my house is sold. Or, it will be as soon as I sign the paperwork and send it back."

"I'm happy for you. This is what you've been waiting for."

She could see he didn't look happy about the news. "I think I'll stay around the area somewhere. I've done a little looking around."

"Have you found a new house?"

Bridget shook her head.

"Life is short. Normally I'd wait for a better time, but I don't want to delay what I have to say. I've never met a woman like you—never had feelings like I've had feelings for you. I know we haven't seen each other for the past weeks and that's only because I guessed that's how you wanted things."

She knew it was time to tell him the complete truth. "I wanted to spend time with you, but the idea of doing that scared me for many reasons."

He drew his eyebrows together. "Like what?"

"It doesn't matter."

"It matters to me. Tell me what scared you."

Because he admitted to having feelings for her, she felt safe to continue, "You're Amish and I'm not. Then there was the rumor about you seeing a young woman."

"Who turned out to be my daughter?"

"Well, I didn't know that, but we're still from different worlds, and that's the line drawn in the sand right there. I can't join the community."

"And I can't leave; this is my life."

Bridget nodded. "I understand. I wouldn't want you to leave."

The baby moved and her eyes opened and she screwed her face up and cried.

"Back to Mom," Dan said with a smile.

"She's hungry. I'll have to feed her."

"Can I call back and see you tomorrow?" he asked.

"I'd like that."

He passed the baby to her. She placed Olivia against her chest, so her head was close to her shoulder while she walked Dan the small distance to the cabin door. Olivia had stopped crying when Dan turned at the door to face Bridget.

"Can I bring you anything when I come back?"

"No, thank you. Ruth's doing some shopping for me tomorrow. I've got enough until then."

He smiled and hesitated as though he didn't want to leave and neither did Bridget want him to leave. When he walked away, Bridget closed the door and then stood a little distance back from the kitchen window where she could watch him.

She knew that he might have asked her to marry him until she said she could never be Amish and live that lifestyle. Being Amish seemed to have its good points, but it had definite bad ones. From living so close to Ruth and Jakob, she saw how close the community was and how they rallied around when anyone was in trouble or needed something done. It was as she imagined the pioneers would have been hundreds of years ago. She'd always believed in God since she was a little girl, but she couldn't see sense in some of the rules the Amish had.

CHAPTER 22

Nevertheless let every one of you in particular so love his wife
even as himself;
and the wife see that she reverence her husband.
Ephesians 5:33

RUTH BROUGHT the shopping to her the next day.

"Thank you, Ruth. I'm so grateful."

"It was nothing. I had to go to the store myself and it was just a few extra things."

"I should be alright to go myself soon when I get organized. Many people have to shop and take a baby with them, so I'll do it too. Would you like a cup of tea?"

"No, thank you." She handed Bridget a parcel.

"What's this?"

"Just a little something for Olivia."

Bridget unwrapped the parcel and inside was a white knitted baby jacket with a hood and baby booties. "Ruth, they're beautiful. Did you knit them?"

"I did."

"They mean so much more, then. Olivia will love them."

Ruth giggled. "I'll have a little peep in at her and then I'll have to do some cooking." Ruth hurried to the room where Olivia was asleep in her bassinet.

After Ruth had gone, Dan knocked on her door.

"Come in." Bridget had thought about Dan the whole night and had imagined the life that Dan, she, and her baby could live together. The thought of her daughter being safely raised in the protective Amish community was appealing. There, her daughter would be safe from so many of the things that children of today's world face. Then again, was it a realistic a choice for her, since she hadn't been raised with their ways?

"Hello, Bridget."

"Hi. Would you like tea or coffee?"

He shook his head.

She sat on the couch and he sat next to her.

"I've got an idea."

"What?"

"Come to my brother's wedding."

"I thought he was married."

He chuckled. "I've got more than one; I told you

that. I've got many. The one who lives closest to me is married, but not Mark. Mark lives in Ohio and his wife is from this community. They knew each other as children and then they were reunited earlier this year."

"Is the wedding going to be close by?"

"Yes, only a few miles from here."

"When?"

"Next month."

"I'd like to see an Amish wedding. Thank you. I'll look forward to it. Is it okay if Olivia comes, too?"

"Of course. And I'd like you to come to the mud sale with me next week Saturday. I know you're tired, but just come with me and we only need stay an hour or so. I just want you to see some of my life."

She nodded. "Your life is a mud sale?"

"Sometimes." He laughed. "There'll be a mix of *Englisch* people and Amish."

"I'd like to take a look."

He smiled and sat a little straighter.

"Are you taking any of your rocking horses to sell?"

"Not to this sale. I donated five in the past year to be auctioned for various charities."

"That's very generous. Have you had any results from the website yet?"

"It's paid for itself already. I got two orders from it this month online, and three people found me and came into the store and bought. That's five in total."

"Wow, that's so good. You should've told me sooner."

"Well, we kind of weren't speaking, or something. I'm not sure what was going on."

She shook her head. "It's like I said, I didn't want to get too close through fear of things turning out weird between us."

"I know." He looked around. "Is Olivia asleep?"

"She is. She was awake most of the night."

"I won't keep you. You'll probably want to get some sleep yourself."

"Yeah, I suppose I should."

"Please call me if you need anything, Bridget. Or if there's anything I can do for you or anything I can bring you."

Bridget smiled at his enthusiasm. "I will."

He stood up. "I'm looking forward to the mud sale."

Bridget stood as well. "Me too. I've heard about them, but I've never been to one. That's where you have auctions to raise money?"

"Yes. We're raising money for the local firefighters, and it'll be an early start."

"How early?"

"Eight."

Bridget pulled a face.

"I'll get here at eight, and there's no hurry. We can get there anytime. It'll go until mid-afternoon."

"I'll be ready. I hope Olivia's sleeping through the night by then."

"If you're too tired, you don't have to come with me."

148

"I'll try. I want to go and see what one's like."

She walked him to the door. He turned around and smiled at her before he headed to his buggy. Something inside her wanted to call him back; she didn't want him to leave.

CHAPTER 23

And the LORD God caused a deep sleep to fall upon Adam, and he slept: and he took one of his ribs, and closed up the flesh instead thereof;
Genesis 2:22

BRIDGET HAD Olivia dressed and ready to go a little before eight o'clock. Olivia had fallen asleep in the middle of nursing and was now in her stroller ready and waiting even though she was asleep.

Is it a mistake, going to the mud sale with him? What would it achieve? Bridget wondered. She knew she had deep feelings for him and was scared to explore those feelings. What would happen if she let go and allowed herself to be carried along by love? Would it be so bad to join the Amish community?

Her usual routine had changed now that Olivia had come along. She no longer took a morning walk because she was too tired in the morning. She'd seen Ruth in the garden yesterday and had mentioned she was going to the mud sale with Dan. The look on Ruth's face had said it all. Ruth was not happy she was spending so much time with Dan.

Dan arrived at eight just like he'd said he would. Bridget pushed the stroller outside the door and closed it behind her.

"Are we taking all of this?" His eyes went to the large diaper bag and then the stroller.

"Yes. The stroller folds up."

He moved closer to get a better look at Olivia. "She's changed and gotten bigger in that short space of time since I last saw her."

"Do you think so? I guess I can't tell because I see her every day. I'm taking her to the clinic tomorrow and then I'll find out how much weight she's put on."

"What would you like me to take?" he asked.

"Can you hold Olivia for a second while I fold up the stroller?"

"I'd love to." He took the baby into his arms, carefully placing her neck in the fold of his elbow. He swayed to and fro while he watched Bridget fold the stroller. "I could've done that; it was easy enough."

"You can carry it to the buggy."

"So, you don't mind if we go in the buggy?"

"Oh, I hadn't thought we could take the car."

"No, we'll take the buggy. I'm determined to show you that it's not too bad."

She giggled and took Olivia from him. "Okay, I'll give it a go."

"That's all I ask." Dan leaned down and picked up the stroller and threw the diaper bag over his shoulder, and then he headed back to his buggy while Bridget and Olivia followed close behind.

ALL THE WAY there in the buggy, Bridget couldn't stop smiling. She felt she was back at the fairgrounds when she was a child, when a horse and cart took the children around the perimeter of the grounds. "This is enjoyable."

"I told you it wouldn't be as bad as you thought."

"I don't know why I resisted going in a buggy for so long."

"It could've had something to do with your morning sickness. I believe you told me months ago that you were queasy."

"That's right. I knew there had to be a reason."

After Dan parked his buggy at the end of a long row of buggies, he helped Bridget out of the car and unfolded the stroller.

"We're blessed to have such a fine day. The sun is shining and there's not a cloud in the sky."

Bridget glanced up at the clear blue sky. It was certainly wonderful to live at the slower pace she'd been living at since she'd been staying in the cabin. Perhaps that's what it would be like if she joined the Amish. Although she'd had a good job, she'd never dreamed of climbing the corporate ladder. She'd been content with the life she'd had with Mattie. She shrugged as a cold shiver ran down her back. She was doing what Mattie said and giving herself a chance at love.

"Are you alright?" he asked.

"Yes. I will be when I wake up properly. I didn't get much sleep last night."

"You didn't have to come."

"I wanted to."

She placed Olivia into the stroller.

"Let me know when you want to leave, Bridget."

"I'll be okay. Are you ready to show me around?"

He smiled at her, and put his hands on the bar of the stroller. "Shall I push?"

She nodded. They walked around, going from stall to stall like a genuine couple. It felt good to have a man by her side again—someone she was happy to be with. The first stall they came to sold chicken corn soup.

"I shouldn't have eaten breakfast. I didn't know there would be so much food here."

"Yeah, I should've mentioned that."

Along the same row was every kind of baked good

that Bridget could have thought of. The smell of freshly baked bread and pastry filled the air.

They moved on to find craftwork including wood-work, needlework, crocheted and knitted items, and patchwork. There was an auction of antique furniture scheduled to start later that day.

"Have we walked around the whole place yet?"

"About halfway."

"Wow. This is my exercise for the week."

"Let's stop and have something to eat over there." He pointed to a tent that was serving tea, coffee and light snacks.

"Okay." On the way over, she glanced at Olivia. "I can't believe she's still asleep. I thought all the walking would've woken her up."

They sat down at a table and Dan headed off to bring back some hot tea.

He brought back two plates of food and two cups of tea on a white plastic tray.

"What's that?" Bridget asked pointing at the food.

"Apple crumble. My mother used to make it and it was my favorite. I've never tasted an apple crumble as good as she used to make. She used some kind of spice to give it a tang, but it wasn't too much."

"She was a good cook?"

"The best. I was still young, but I remember some of the things she used to cook. You remind me of her little bit."

Bridget giggled. "That's the first time someone told me I remind them of their mother, and I'm not sure if that is a compliment."

"It's very much a compliment. My mother's hair was fair like yours and she had a kind and gentle nature like you. Even though she had so many children, she made the time to spend some with each one of us."

"You remember that?"

He nodded. "She was a caring woman. It would've been nice if she could've lived longer."

"We've both had losses in our lives," she said.

"It's a part of life, I suppose. Everyone's bound to lose someone they love sooner or later. It's odd to think I didn't even know I had a daughter and then she appeared fully grown in front of me." He placed some apple crumble in his mouth.

"How are things going between you and Lacey now?"

"We're talking a little bit more. I think when she gets to know me a little better, she'll realize I didn't stay away from her deliberately when she was growing up."

"But you've told her that already, haven't you?"

He nodded. "I'm hoping she'll come around. As you pointed out, she's only twenty, which is quite young and very often young people don't see reason."

"It wasn't until I had Olivia that I started seeing my parents in a new light. I don't think I saw them as people before; I saw them as parents and not as real people. Now I see that they do care about me. They even wanted Olivia and me to move in with them." She shook her head. "It's hard to explain. I never thought my parents were perfect but now I'm actually seeing them as people and I like them a whole lot more." She pushed her fork into the apple crumble and popped a portion into her mouth. "Mmm, this is delicious."

"It's always been my favorite. My mother's was much better, though. I hope that Lacey and I can get along better before she has a child. I don't want to wait that long for her to accept me."

"Don't forget she'd be grieving the loss of her mother. It can't be easy, and then finding out about you adds another whole emotional upheaval. It seems reasonable that she places some blame onto you."

His eyebrows drew together. "What did I do?"

"Nothing, but she's hurting and needs to blame someone and you're the closest person to blame."

He pulled his mouth to one side. "What should I do?"

"Wait. Be there and wait patiently."

"I guess I can do that."

BRIDGET THOUGHT it would be good to get home before she had to feed Olivia. She was still breast-feeding and didn't know where she'd be able to do that at the mud sale. Thankfully, Olivia was still asleep when Bridget asked Dan to take them home.

"I've had a lovely day," she said as they walked back to the buggy.

As soon as they got to the buggy and Olivia had to be lifted out to fold the stroller, she woke. She didn't cry at first, but Bridget knew it wouldn't be long before she was crying for another feeding.

When they neared home, Olivia had found her lungs and was howling.

"Thank you for bringing us to the mud sale. It was lovely."

"I'm glad you both came to have a look."

When he drew closer to the cabin, there was a black car parked next to Bridget's.

"Do you have a visitor?"

She stared over at the car while jiggling Olivia, trying to lull her and give her some comfort, and then she saw Nat getting out of his car. Nat leaned against the door with his arms folded, staring at the buggy.

"Oh no! My parents promised they wouldn't tell him where I'm staying."

Olivia howled louder.

"Who is he?"

"It's a long story."

Dan stopped the buggy and got the stroller out, along with the diaper bag. Bridget stepped down from the buggy with Olivia still in her arms.

Nat walked over and she introduced the two men.

"Will you be okay, Bridget?"

"Yeah, I'll be fine. Thank you."

"I'll help her from here," Nat said taking the folded stroller and bag from him.

With Olivia still crying, she turned to say goodbye again to Dan, but he was already at his buggy. She entered the house with Nat behind her.

"Just drop the things there by the door thanks, Nat."

"Your parents told me you had the baby."

"Yes, a few weeks ago now. Will you excuse me while I feed her?"

"Yeah sure."

"Make yourself comfortable and there's food in the fridge if you're hungry."

Bridget hurried to the bedroom so she could feed her baby in private. Nat had chosen the worse time to show up. She'd have to tell him she had no interest in him, but had she misled him in the past? After she'd gone over everything in her mind since Mattie had died, she knew she'd done nothing to have Nat think she was interested in him. Perhaps he was holding onto the past, her feelings before he'd dumped her for Crystal.

Twenty minutes later, Olivia had been fed and had fallen back to sleep. After Bridget had placed her in the crib, she closed the door and walked out to talk to Nat. "I'm sorry. I should've told you how long that was going to take." She saw that he'd been reading one of her romance books.

He closed the book and held it in his hand. "You believe all this stuff?"

"No. I did once—I guess."

"I suppose you blame me for that?"

Bridget laughed. "No. Well… maybe. It doesn't matter now. That's ancient history."

He stood up. "It doesn't have to be."

"Yes, it does."

"We could take up where we left off."

She shook her head. "That would never work."

"What about your daughter?"

"What do you mean?'

"It'll be hard to be a single parent. Are you up for that?"

"I'll have to be. It's not what I would've chosen, but I wasn't given a choice. Do you want tea or coffee, or a cold drink perhaps?"

"What happened to you, Bridget?"

"What do you mean? Do you expect me to fall into your arms now after you dumped me and broke my heart in the past?"

"So you loved me once." A smug grin settled on his face.

"I thought so, but it can't have been real."

"We can start over."

She put both of her hands on the small kitchen counter where she'd moved so there'd be something between them. "I don't want to start over, Nat. I hope you didn't come all this way hoping something would happen between us. Did you?"

"You know how I've always felt about you. That's why I bought the house next to your parents. I knew I'd see you every time you came home."

She stared at him, scarcely believing his words. It was flattering for him to buy the house next to her parents, but at the same time, it was also weird. He was the one who'd dumped her for something new and shiny. How could she ever trust him again? But a man like Dan; she knew she'd always be able to trust him.

"I'm serious about you, Bridget." He walked toward her.

She shook her head. "We were children back then. Too many years have passed. I'm not the same person I was back then. Any woman would love to have a man like you, Nat." She tried to build him up before she asked him to leave. "But I can't be that woman for you."

"I'm serious about you, Bridget. Won't you forgive me? I might even consider marrying you one day."

Bridget tried to hold back her laughter. She tried to appeal to his shallow self to turn him away. "I couldn't be everything you want in a woman. I look awful in a bikini now that I've got dreadful stretch marks, and..." she looked down at her chest. "I'm sagging everywhere. A man as handsome as you needs a woman who is beautiful. And it would be hard for you to raise another man's child. Olivia would always be wanting to know about her 'real' father."

"I didn't think of all those things." He smiled. "You always were the one with the level head. I hoped it would work. I had hoped we'd be able to get back what we had. You were good to me and you really were the only woman who cared about me. I was stupid to throw that all away."

"These things happen for a reason, I guess. If that hadn't happened, I wouldn't have Olivia. And, you'll meet your perfect woman and she'll be so perfect, it will be so far beyond what we once had together, that you'll be amazed."

"Do you think so?"

She nodded. "I know so."

He smiled and his fingertips touched his square jawline. "Do you need anything, Bridget—money, or anything?"

"I'm fine. I have everything I need."

He looked around the cabin. "Bit of a dump, isn't it?"

"It's fine. It suits me." She didn't tell him she was going to buy a house soon.

"I'll go, then. It's a long drive. It was good to see your baby, and congratulations."

"Thank you, Nat. I'll walk you out."

WHEN SHE WALKED BACK into the house, she was

anxious to explain to Dan who Nat was. She didn't want him getting the wrong idea, but she'd have to wait until Monday, as he'd be at his Amish worship meeting the next day. Going to his house the next day in the afternoon didn't seem appropriate, so she'd stop into his shop on Monday morning. With a big effort, she chose to put it out of her mind until then.

CHAPTER 24

Keep yourselves in the love of God, looking for the mercy of our Lord Jesus Christ unto eternal life.
Jude 1:21

PULLING the baby carrier out of her car wasn't an easy thing to do. Bridget couldn't quite get the hang of it and once she'd unclipped it, she hoped she'd be able to clip it back into the frame. Once it was free, it was a good basket to carry her baby in. She looped the carrier over her arm, and headed to Dan's store, which was only two shops down the road from where she'd been lucky enough to find a parking spot.

Bridget walked into the shop and when she saw that he had customers, she wandered around the shop and looked at various things as though she were a customer. When his customers left, he slowly walked over to her.

"This is a nice surprise. I didn't expect to see you here today."

"I just want to thank you again for taking me to the mud sale. It was a shame I couldn't have stayed longer."

"When Olivia gets older you'll be able to do more things, I guess." He leaned over and looked in the carrier. "Fast asleep."

"She always falls asleep in the car for some reason. I should try driving her around at night."

He laughed. "Is she having trouble going to sleep?"

"She has no trouble getting to sleep; she has trouble staying asleep, particularly at night."

"Are you on your way somewhere?"

This was more awkward than she thought it would be; she had no reason to be there. He hadn't invited her there, and right at this moment, she didn't know if he wanted her there. "I wanted to explain who the man was when you dropped me off on Saturday."

He shook his head and stepped back slightly. "You don't owe me any explanations."

"I just didn't want you to get the wrong idea."

"Who was he?"

She breathed out heavily. "It's a long story."

"I believe you told me that on Saturday. Do you have time for coffee or tea? I could get us one?"

"I've got time, but I really don't feel like anything. I'll get you one if you want one."

"No, I'm fine. Come through to the back."

Now that he'd asked her into his workshop area, she felt a bit more comfortable.

She sat down and began her story. "Well, he was my first boyfriend. I thought we would get married. Matthew, the man I married—you've probably heard me call him Mattie—had a girlfriend called Crystal. What happened is that Crystal and Nat got together and basically cheated on me and Mattie."

"Oh, that's not nice. Then how did you and Mattie end up marrying?"

"We'd always been very good friends and with us both being dumped at the same time it gave us something else in common, and then we just drifted together. I guess it doesn't sound very romantic."

"And that's important to you—romance?"

"I think every woman likes a bit of romance every now and again. I'm not consumed by the thought of it, but love and romance add a bit of spice to life."

He smiled. "That's true, they do."

"You think so too?"

He nodded. "That's kind of how I felt ever since you moved into Ruth's cabin. It was hard for me those weeks that I had to stay away from you."

"You didn't have to."

"Things were awkward between us." His smile faded.

"I didn't want them to be."

"What is it that you want, Bridget?"

"I want to be happy. And more than that, I want Olivia to be happy and have a good life."

"Every parent wants the best for their child. But I asked what you want, Bridget. You said you want to be happy?"

"That's not all. I want to feel safe and at some stage, I would like a family."

"So you're not against the idea of marrying again?"

She shook her head "I'm not against it at all. Mattie would've wanted me to get married again. We talked a little bit, in the early days when he joined the Marines, what might happen if he didn't come home."

"I know we've never talked about this, but I get the feeling that you believe in God or have some kind of respect for the Amish faith."

"I went to Sunday school when I was growing up. And when I was a teenager, I was very interested in the Amish. I like how your way of life is simple and I don't know what the word is, but kind of untainted from all the horrible things happening in the world all the time."

"And now?"

"What do you mean?"

"You are speaking as though you don't like the idea of that kind of lifestyle now. Or, perhaps you think it's not for you?"

"I think I'm liking it more and more." She looked directly into his eyes and he reached over and took hold of her hand.

"Bridget, I've liked you for a long time." He gave a small chuckle. "I guess it's only a short time really—only a few months, but I feel like I've known you for a long time. Bridget, you're the woman I've been waiting for. I need to ask you something."

She leaned forward. "Yes?"

Right at that moment, someone coming into the store interrupted them.

Dan craned his neck looking out into the store. "It's Deirdre. She has to have the worst timing ever," he whispered. "We might have to continue this conversation another time."

Bridget stood up and took hold of her baby carrier. "Well, I need to do some errands before Olivia wakes up again."

"If I don't see you before, I'll see you when I come to collect you for my brother's wedding. Don't you forget about that, now."

"I won't." Bridget walked out of the back room and came face-to-face with Deirdre who was pleased to see both her and the baby.

They chatted about Olivia. All Bridget wanted to do was get out of the store as fast as she could. When she finally left, she walked quickly to her car because she felt tears welling. She attached the baby carrier to the fixture in the back seat and luckily the whole thing clipped into place on the first try. Bridget sat in the driver's seat and sobbed. Was it really okay for her to want a relationship with Dan? Was he the one, her soul mate?

She was sure that Dan had been going to ask her to marry him and then it had all been ruined. Why didn't he say he would come by later that day to finish off what he'd been going to say? Why was he waiting until his brother's wedding, which was still weeks away?

Were the Amish always slow like that, or was it only Dan? Bridget was the kind of person to get things done right away. Perhaps Dan was a cautious person who plodded through life at a slow pace.

Twisting the rear view mirror to see herself, she wiped mascara smudges from beneath her eyes. It had taken Dan awhile to get that website going; he'd thought about it for years but hadn't acted on his intention. It was hard for her to wait to hear what he had to say, but she'd have to wait for him to be ready to say it—she had no other choice.

THAT AFTERNOON when Olivia was asleep, Bridget looked out her window to see Ruth banging dust out of the floor rugs. She stepped outside the cabin just as Ruth looked over.

"How are you doing today, Bridget?" Ruth called out.

"I'm feeling better every day. I'm a little less tired and I'm getting a little more sleep too, so I suppose that's why."

"That's good. Sleeping better is she?" Ruth left her rugs and walked over to her.

"I don't know that she's sleeping better, but I'm sleeping more through the day when she's asleep. I've given up trying to sleep all through the night."

"That's a wise idea." Ruth stared into her eyes. "Have you been crying? Your eyes are all red."

Bridget forced a laugh. "I will admit to being a bit emotional. Everything seems to be escalating. Things that normally wouldn't upset me upset me a lot."

"That's quite normal; don't worry about it one little bit."

"Really, is that normal?"

"Very normal. Don't be concerned."

"Do you have time for a cup of tea, Ruth?"

"I'd love one."

Once they were settled with a cup of tea in hand, Bridget asked about the process of becoming Amish. Ruth told her about taking the instructions, which were lessons the bishop gave new people, and most single Amish people were to live with a family for a few months to gain an understanding of the lifestyle.

"You can stay with me if you decide you want to become Amish. Is that what this is about?"

"I don't know. I guess I'm thinking about it, that's all. It's good to know what it involves."

"It's not something to take lightly."

"Oh, I know that and I wouldn't make the step unless I was going to follow through with it."

"Does this have anything to do with Dan?"

Bridget smiled and opened her mouth to speak when Ruth said, "You should do this only for yourself and not because you have your eyes on a man."

Staring at Ruth, she wanted to be cross with her for being so stern, but she was right. If Bridget were going to make big decisions that would affect not only her life but also Olivia's life, she'd have to take her feelings for Dan out of the equation. "I've got a lot to think about."

Ruth nodded.

CHAPTER 25

And he saith unto me, Write, Blessed are they which are called
unto the marriage supper of the Lamb. And he saith unto me,
These are the true sayings of God.
Revelation 19:9

THE DAY of Dan's brother's wedding came and Bridget and Olivia were dressed and waiting. Rather than her normal clothing of loose pants, Bridget wore a dress out of respect. She knew the Amish didn't like a woman to wear pants, which they considered men's clothing.

When she saw the buggy draw close, she headed out the door with Olivia in her stroller and the large diaper bag. She hoped he'd remember what he had been about to say to her the last time he'd seen her. And if he didn't, perhaps she wasn't as important to him as she hoped that she was.

He jumped down from the buggy and waved to her as he walked toward her with his usual wide grin.

"Morning," he said.

"Good morning. It looks like it's going to be a beautiful day for it."

He glanced up at the sky. "A perfect day." Glancing down at Olivia, he said, "She's asleep."

"Not for long."

"Can we go inside for a moment?"

"Yes. Is there anything wrong?" She immediately thought that he was going to uninvite her to the wedding. Perhaps he'd chosen Deirdre over her.

"Nothing's wrong."

She pushed the stroller inside and then he closed the door behind them. He took the diaper bag from her and placed it on the nearby kitchen counter.

"I want to speak with you before the wedding. There will be a lot of people there and they'll all want to know who you are and why you're there."

"I don't have to go; it's okay."

"I want you to go. With me." He breathed out heavily. "I'm not good at this. Bridget, will you consider marrying me?"

Relief washed over her. He felt the same as she. "You want to marry me?"

He nodded. "I know it'll mean changing your life

and Olivia's life and I know you might not want to do that. But, I couldn't go another day without at least letting you know how I feel about you. I'd love it if you agreed to marry me." He took her hand and held it.

"I *will* marry you." It felt right. Now she knew the reason she'd come to the cabin.

"Seriously? You will? Don't you want to think about it?"

She laughed. "No. I know how I feel. I would love to marry you."

He took her into his strong arms and held her close. "You've made me a very happy man. We'll have to speak to the bishop today and set up a meeting to discuss everything. Today, we should keep this to ourselves apart from telling the bishop."

"Okay." Bridget was pleased he was making plans already. He was breaking out of his normal plodding behavior. She closed her eyes and placed her head on his shoulder while they held each other in silence. All she could hear were the beating of his heart and the early morning birds chirping in the trees outside as she breathed in the smell of his freshly laundered white shirt. Finally, she was at peace and knew where she belonged.

He stepped back after a moment and looked into her eyes. "I've got so many plans to make. I have to fix up my old house and you'll have to learn some Pennsylvania Dutch and so many other things."

"I'm ready," Bridget said.

"I'm a very happy man today," he whispered as he pulled her close once more.

When Olivia whimpered, Bridget said, "Oh no, she's awake. She should go to sleep again in the buggy."

Dan chuckled. "Come on. We've got a wedding to go to. And then the next one we go to after that might be our own."

BRIDGET SAT through the wedding service at the bride's home with Olivia in her arms. All the while, she imagined what it would be like to have an Amish wedding. Her first wedding had been a traditional wedding with a beautiful long white dress and a three-tiered white cake. Never in her wildest dreams had she thought she'd marry a second time, and never ever to an Amish man. When she turned to look at the other guests, she saw Deirdre. How would Deirdre take the news when she heard that she was going to marry Dan?

Deirdre could've been a good friend, but now she would most likely feel as though Bridget had betrayed her. She closed her eyes and prayed that Deirdre wouldn't be hurt by the news.

IT WASN'T TOO MUCH LATER in the day that Deirdre walked over and joined Bridget at one of the food tables. Dan was off talking to someone on the other side of the yard.

"Bridget, it's so nice to see you here. I thought it was you when you came into the house."

"Hello, Deirdre."

"Look how big Olivia has gotten. May I hold her?"

Bridget giggled. "Please do. My arms need a rest."

Deirdre sat down next to her after having taken hold of Olivia.

"I've got something to tell you," Deirdre whispered to Bridget.

"What?"

"Andrew and I are getting married."

"That's great news! I'm so happy for you. When are you getting married?"

"Soon. We're announcing it in the next few weeks."

"That's so good."

"I'm pleased. I've grown to love him. You were right about marrying your best friend."

Bridget grimaced. "I'm not one to give advice."

"It was my decision."

"Good," Bridget said still hoping Deirdre wouldn't be angry with her when she found out. She couldn't tell Bridget or anyone until the time was right. It was possible that the bishop might not accept her into the community—anyway, it was far too early to tell anyone.

Deirdre looked down at Olivia who had nodded off to sleep. "It must be so good to have a baby."

"It is. It's something you have to experience to

know what it's like. It's a true miracle—that's how I felt when I saw her for the first time. I couldn't believe that she came from me."

Deirdre smiled and Bridget really wanted to tell her the good news, but she couldn't.

Six months later, Bridget and Dan were standing in front of the bishop in Ruth and Jakob's home, and they had just been pronounced married.

Bridget had moved from the cabin into Ruth's home. She'd learned the Amish ways, taken the instructions and been baptized. Now she was an Amish woman and felt as though she'd come home. Ruth and Deirdre were now her closest friends.

Dan held her hand, and she looked into his eyes. The day before, he'd told her he loved her. In her heart, Bridget knew he loved her, but it had been hard for him to say. It filled her heart with joy when she'd heard it.

More than anything, Bridget felt safe and protected.

As they walked out of Ruth's house hand-in-hand, Bridget looked up to see all the tables that were spread with food. This was her wedding day and she was going to enjoy it. Even her parents had come and were both happy to see her get married. They liked Dan's steadfast nature and ready smile.

"Thank you for marrying me, Bridget," Dan whispered in her ear.

She turned slightly to look into his eyes. "I'm so happy."

They sat down at the wedding table, and Bridget's first marriage to Mattie flashed through her head. She'd been blessed to find two wonderful men in her lifetime when many a woman didn't find even one. The love for each man had been different. With Mattie, it was more of a friendship kind of love, and with Dan, it was as though they were two pieces of a jigsaw puzzle that fitted neatly together.

God had orchestrated events for them to find each other. Bridget found out weeks ago that Ruth had no idea how a leaflet advertising her cabin had found its way into a small café in Pottstown.

When she heard a yell, Bridget looked over to see Olivia with Deirdre. Bridget smiled, knowing that Olivia was the first of many children that she and Dan would have. They both wanted many and Dan was already forging ahead with plans for extending his house to accommodate them—and Max. Yes, Dan had turned from a plodder into someone who made things happen.

Bridget closed her eyes briefly and thanked God for choosing her to be the woman who would marry Dan Lindenlaub.

And Jesus said unto them, Because of your unbelief: for verily I

say unto you, If ye have faith as a grain of mustard seed, ye shall say unto this mountain, Remove hence to yonder place; and it shall remove; and nothing shall be impossible unto you.
Matthew 17:19-21

Thank you for your interest in Amish Widow's Escape.
The next in the series is:
Book 12 Amish Widow's Christmas

WIDOWED AND PREGNANT AMISH WOMAN, Sarah Kurtz, is in dire financial circumstances.

Relief comes unexpectedly when her late uncle leaves her his income-producing farm in Sugarcreek.

After Sarah's baby is born, she leaves Lancaster County and moves to her new home, unaware there is a long-term tenant living in the adjoining grossdaddi haus.

When she meets her disagreeable neighbor, Joshua Byler, her irritation with him is softened by his two children.

Not wanting her daughter to be raised with one parent and no siblings as she was, Sarah knows the only solution is to marry again.

With Christmas looming, will Sarah find her prayers are answered?

Or will she let Joshua Byler stand in her way of happiness?

OTHER BOOKS IN THE EXPECTANT
AMISH WIDOWS SERIES

ABOUT SAMANTHA PRICE

Samantha Price wrote stories from a young age, but it wasn't until later in life that she took up writing full time. Formally an artist, she exchanged her paintbrush for the computer and, many best-selling book series later, has never looked back.

Samantha is happiest on her computer lost in the world of her characters.

She is best known for the Ettie Smith Amish Mysteries series and the Expectant Amish Widows series.

To learn more about Samantha Price and her books visit:

www.samanthapriceauthor.com

Samantha Price loves to hear from her readers. Connect with her at:

    samanthaprice333@gmail.com

    www.facebook.com/SamanthaPriceAuthor

    Follow Samantha Price on BookBub

    Twitter @ AmishRomance

35094077R00105

Made in the USA
Lexington, KY
31 March 2019